The Classical Analogy between Speech and Music and Its Transmission in Carolingian Music Theory

MEDIEVAL AND RENAISSANCE
TEXTS AND STUDIES

VOLUME 400

The Classical Analogy between Speech and Music and Its Transmission in Carolingian Music Theory

By
Blair Sullivan

ACMRS
(Arizona Center for Medieval and Renaissance Studies)
Tempe, Arizona
2011

Published by ACMRS (Arizona Center for Medieval and Renaissance Studies)
Tempe, Arizona
© 2011 by the Arizona Board of Regents for Arizona State University
All Rights Reserved.

Library of Congress Cataloging-in-Publication Data

Sullivan, Blair.
 The classical analogy between speech and music and its transmission in
Carolingian music theory / by Blair Sullivan.
     p. cm. -- (Medieval and renaissance texts and studies ; v. 400)
 Includes bibliographical references.
 ISBN 978-0-86698-448-5 (alk. paper)
1. Music theory--History--500-1400. 2. Musical notation--Early works to
1800. 3. Music and language. I. Title.
 ML174.S84 2011
 781.09'021--dc23
                                                            2011040771

This book is made to last. It is set in Adobe Caslon Pro,
smyth-sewn and printed on acid-free paper to library specifications.
Printed in the United States of America.

TABLE OF CONTENTS

INTRODUCTION

In this book I study a particular type of postulated similarity: analogies between the structure of the sound of human speech and the structure of musical sound. "Grammatical" analogies, as I call them, appear in four of the ninth-century music handbooks or treatises that transmit the essential elements of our knowledge of contemporary Carolingian music theory and practice: Aurelian of Réôme's *Musica disciplina*; Hucbald of St. Amand's *Musica*; and the anonymous *Musica enchiriadis* and its frequent, also anonymous, companion in the manuscript tradition, *Scolica enchiriadis*.[1] I address fundamental questions about the ancient origins of the theoretical association between speech and music and statements of structural similarity between the two, and examine the implications of the use of this traditional association by ninth-century Carolingian scholars in their efforts to investigate the essential nature of music, to identify the fundamental principles that govern its appearances, and to apply those principles to the study and practice of contemporary liturgical music.

The energy and creativity of Carolingian educational advances and reforms throughout the ninth century have been well documented and studied.[2] In particular, for the scholarly consideration of liturgical music—both through

---

[1] With regard to the dating of these treatises, Barbara Haggh argues that the text of Aurelian's *Musica disciplina* was written between 843 and 856 and then revised between 856 and 861: Barbara Haggh, "Traktat *Musica disciplina* Aureliana Reomensis: Proweniencja i datowanie," *Muzyka* 2 (2000): 25–78. Yves Chartier tentatively dates Hucbald's *Musica* to 883–884: *L'oeuvre musicale d'Hucbald de Saint-Amand*, ed. Yves Chartier, Cahiers d'Études Médiévales, Cahier Spécial 5 (Montreal, 1995), 76–77. Raymond Erickson writes that both *Musica* and *Scolica enchiriadis* undoubtedly have complicated histories involving several stages of evolution possibly beginning in the first half of the ninth century, but that it seems likely that the standard versions known today are from much later in the century: *Musica and Scolica enchiriadis*, ed. and trans. Raymond Erickson (New Haven and London, 1995), xxi–xii; and idem, "Musica enchiriadis, Scolica enchiriadis," in *Grove Music Online. Oxford Music Online*, http://www.oxfordmusiconline.com/subscriber/article/grove/music/19405. See also C. Meyer, *Les traités de musique*, Typologie des sources du Moyen Âge occidental 85 (Turnhout, 2001).

[2] For an excellent summary, see John Contreni, "The Carolingian Renaissance: Education and Literary Culture," in *The New Cambridge Medieval History*, vol. 2, *c.700–c.900*, ed. Rosamond McKitterick (Cambridge, 1995) 709–57; on the liturgy in particular, see Yitzhak Hen, *The Royal Patronage of Liturgy in Frankish Gaul* (Woodbridge, 2001).

traditional theory and in contemporary practice—Carolingian teachers and writers had available to them Pythagorean-Platonic harmonic theory, principally as transmitted by Martianus Capella, Boethius, Cassiodorus, and Isidore of Seville; the Aristoxenian tradition of phenomenalism in the study of musical sound; and grammatical theory in the writings of late Latin grammarians such as Donatus, Diomedes, and Priscian.[3] In this study, I use the grammatical analogies in these Carolingian music handbooks as a starting point for my examination of the interplay of harmonic tradition, grammatical theory, and liturgical practice which led to their production.

Carolingian Use of Grammatical Analogies

The specific grammatical analogies I examine include the following two examples from *Musica enchiriadis*:

1. The first sentence of chapter 1, describing the objects of investigation:

    Just as the elementary and indivisible constituents of speech (*vox articulata*) are letters, from which syllables are composed, and in turn nouns and verbs, and finally the complete text of a discourse, so the notes (*phthongi*) which are called sounds (*soni*) in Latin, are the basis of musical sound, and the content of all music can ultimately be reduced to them.[4]

2. From chapter 10, "About the Symphonies," introducing the musical intervals of the octave, the perfect fifth, and the perfect fourth:

    Not all of the notes described above blend together equally pleasantly nor are they concordant in song when joined together in any way whatsoever. Just as letters, if joined together at random, often will not fit together properly (*concordare*) as syllables and words, so in music only certain intervals

---

[3] On medieval reception of ancient music theory, see Calvin M. Bower, "The Transmission of Ancient Music Theory into the Middle Ages," in *The Cambridge History of Western Music Theory*, ed. Thomas Christensen (Cambridge, 2002), 136–67; and Charles M. Atkinson, *The Critical Nexus: Tone-System, Mode, and Notation in Early Medieval Music* (New York, 2008), esp. chap. 2, "The Reception of Ancient Texts in the Carolingian Era."

[4] *Musica et Scolica enchiriadis una cum aliquibus tractatulis adiunctis*, ed. Hans Schmid (henceforth Schmid) (Munich, 1981), 3: "Sicut vocis articulatae elementariae atque individuae partes sunt litterae, ex quibus compositae syllabae rursus componunt verba et nomina eaque perfectae orationis textum, sic canorae vocis ptongi, qui Latine dicuntur soni, origines sunt et totius musicae continentia in eorum ultimam resolutionem desinit." Unless stated otherwise, the English translations are my own.

are able to produce symphonies. A symphony is a sweet singing together of different notes joined to one another.[5]

Each excerpt postulates a specific structural similarity between music and speech:

1. Both the sound of human speech—discourse, which is composed of words, which are in turn composed of syllables—and the sound of music can be reduced to and put together from a finite set of irreducible and distinguishable constituents or elements: letters[6] and notes, respectively.

2. Musical notes, like letters of the alphabet, cannot be joined at random: certain combinations of letters "harmonize" as syllables and words, and certain combinations of notes produce the perfect consonances.

The operative idea is that music—that is, the music that is properly studied as *musica disciplina*—is in many important respects like speech; and this very similarity authorizes the study of the theory and practice of music to proceed, when convenient, along the well-established lines used to describe and analyze human speech. The two citations from *Musica enchiriadis* each illustrate a specific aspect of that hypothetical similarity.

A third type of analogy, having to do with the physical material of musical sound, appears in these handbooks. For example, in chapter 15 of his *Musica* the writer and teacher Hucbald of Saint-Amand (840?–930) describes the particular musical pitches which constitute the gamut of musical sounds (*series sonorum*) that can properly be used for melody:

> These sounds, because they are elements, were considered by the ancients to be the proper beginnings for the study of music and were called by them *phthongi*. These were not just any sounds—for example, the sounds of inanimate objects or the cries of irrational animals—but only those that could be measured and determined by calculable quantities and could be used for melody; these they established as the most certain foundation for all song. It is for this reason that they called them elements or *phthongi*, because just as all the variety of speech can be expressed through its elements, the letters, and anything that can be said can be expressed by them, so also

---

[5] Schmid, 23: "Praemissae voces non omnes aeque suaviter sibi miscentur nec quoquo modo iunctae concordabiles in cantu reddunt effectus. Ut litterae, si inter se passim iungantur, sepe nec verbis nec syllabis concordabunt copulandis, sic in musica quaedam certa sunt intervalla, quae symphonias possint efficere. Est autem symphonia vocum disparium inter se iunctarum dulcis concentus."

[6] That is, the sounded and theoretically, if not actually, phonemic set of letters.

through their ingenuity the ancients have taken care that the melodies in this immense class have only certain beginnings, which are subject to fixed rules and which permit anything that should be sung to be sung without error and allow nothing to be included that is not perfectly intelligible.[7]

An etymology of the term *phthongi* follows immediately as the opening sentence of the next chapter:

They are called *phthongi* from ΑΠΟ ΤΟΥ ΦΘΕΓΓΕϹΘΑΙ [from to utter a sound], by analogy to speaking, for just as words are expressed by means of intelligible speech, sounds enter the mind by means of these *phthongi* . . .[8]

In these two excerpts, Hucbald supports the legitimacy of the selected set of musical elements and the etymology of the special term which designates these elements—separating them from the masses of undifferentiated and unmeasurable sounds—by means of analogical references to the elements of human speech and, of course, to the authority of antiquity.

The use of analogies of this type by Carolingian writers on the subject of *musica disciplina* is well known, and, for the most part, the immediate sources of the analogies have been identified.[9] But the undeniable fact that they carried the

---

[7] *L'oeuvre musicale d'Hucbald de Saint-Amand*, ed. Chartier (henceforth Chartier), 152: "Sonos quibus per quedam veluti elementa ad musicam prisci estimaverunt ingrediendum greco nomine ptongos appellare voluerunt, idest non qualescumque sonos, ut puta quarumlibet insensibilium rerum, aut certe inrationabilium voces animalium, sed eos tantum, quos rationabili discretos ac determinatos quantitate, quique melodiae apti existerent, ipsi certissima totium cantilenae fundamenta iecerunt. Vnde et elementa uel ptongos eosdem nuncuparunt, quod scilicet, quemadmodum litterarum elementis sermonum cuncta multiplicitas coartatur, et quicquid dici potest, per eas digeritur, ita sollerti procurauerunt industria, ut inmensitas cantilenarum quaedam haberet exordia, et ipsa certo moderamine comprehensa, per quae quicquid canendum foret, sine ullo errore procederet, nihilque in eis esset quod non omni prorsus rationabilitate uigeret."

[8] Chartier, 152: "Dicti autem ptongi ΑΠΟ ΤΟΥ ΦΘΕΓΓΕϹΘΑΙ quasi a similitudine loquendi, quod quemadmodum locutione intelligibilia uerba redduntur, ita his sub intellectum decidunt soni . . ."

[9] See, for example, Nancy Phillips, "*Musica* and *Scolica enchiriadis*: The Literary, Theoretical, and Musical Sources" (Ph.D. diss., New York University, 1984), 273–323; eadem, "Classical and Late Latin Sources for Ninth-Century Treatises on Music," in *Music Theory and Its Sources: Antiquity and the Middle Ages*, ed. André Barbera (Notre Dame, 1990), 100–36; eadem, "Music," in *Medieval Latin*, ed. F. A. C. Mantello and A. G. Rigg (Washington, DC, 1996), 296–306; and Blair Sullivan, "Grammar and Harmony: The Written Representation of Sound in Carolingian Treatises" (Ph.D. diss., University of California, Los Angeles, 1994), 32–42. For a discussion of the use of "grammatical models" in medieval music theory treatises, see Calvin M. Bower, "The Grammatical Model of Musical Understanding in the Middle Ages," in *Hermeneutics and*

weight of the authority of their likely sources—Boethius, Calcidius, and others—explains very little. Other than noting their presence in these treatises and identifying various obvious or subtle examples of intertextuality, no one has yet addressed fundamental questions about the ancient origins of these statements of structural similarity between speech and music and the implications of their ultimate use by Carolingian scholars to conceptualize musical sound.

The analogies I have quoted are carefully and strategically placed within their respective treatises. For example, the first analogy from *Musica enchiriadis* opens the treatise, and it is logical that a presentation of the theory and practice of music would begin with an explanation of what is going to be studied. But evidently it was not considered sufficient simply to elaborate the first principles of musical sound; from the outset the anonymous compiler of this handbook follows the model of treatises on grammar which were well known in the Carolingian ninth century. Donatus's *Ars grammatica*, for example, begins, "The letter is the smallest part of speech (*vox articulata*)."[10] Similarly Priscian, in his *Institutio grammatica*, opens his discussion of letters by noting that "the letter is the smallest part of composite speech."[11] Thus the placement of this well-elaborated analogy at the opening of *Musica enchiriadis* explicitly uses the authority and methodology of the body of knowledge associated with grammatical theory to justify the decision to begin the study of musical sound with a consideration of individual pitches, the "smallest parts" of musical sound. And, in general, these analogies appear to be placed so as to invoke that authority at points in the exposition of harmonic theory where intuition and experience might point in various directions, but a specific proposition requires justification. In every one of these examples the prior authority of grammatical theory is clear, and, through the use of analogy, the methodology of grammatical theory provides a basis for the extension of knowledge to another discipline, in this case, music theory.

Medieval Culture, ed. Patrick J. Gallacher and Helen Damico (Albany, 1989), 133–45. Mathias Bielitz, *Musik und Grammatik* (Munich, 1977) remains a useful survey. See also Jan Ziolkowski, *Nota Bene: Reading Classics and Writing Melodies in the Early Middle Ages* (Turnhout, 2007), esp. 65–67, 76–77, 79, 81–83, 86.

[10] Donatus, *Ars Grammatica*, ed. H. Keil, Grammatici Latini, 7 vols. (Leipzig, 1855–1880), 4:367: "Littera est pars minima vocis articulatae."

[11] Priscian, *Institutio grammatica*, ed. H. Keil, Grammatici Latini 2:6: "Litera est pars minima vocis compositae . . ."

Analogy as a Methodological Paradigm

In the most general terms, an analogy is a statement that "a" is to "b" as "c" is to "d"; in symbols a : b :: c : d.[12] Analogies can of course be verbal as well as symbolic, for example, the statement "Puppy is to dog as kitten is to cat." The symbolic analogy a : b :: c : d implies, following standard algebraic procedure, a number of permutations:

a : c :: b : d

c : a :: d : b

b : a :: d : c

But verbal analogies have what is known as an implied or intended directionality. That is, the statement that "puppy is to dog as kitten is to cat" does not mean the same thing as the statement that "puppy is to kitten as dog is to cat"; in fact, its meaning is not immediately clear. Or, to bring the discussion directly to the case at hand, the statement, in its simplest terms, that "note is to music as letter is to speech" has a specific directionality built into it by its author. That directionality is violated if the terms are exchanged according to the rules of algebra: the statement that "note is to letter as music is to speech" calls for a completely different interpretation. In technical terms, a statement of similarity postulates a relationship between a relatum, something which is already known, and a referent, something which is currently under investigation. Thus, in the statement "note is to music as letter is to speech," the referent is music — which is currently under investigation — and the relatum is speech, the properties of which have been investigated previously and firmly established.

A verbal analogy, such as the one between music and speech, is a special type of metaphor: a systematic mapping of knowledge from one domain into another such that a system of relations that holds among the objects of the referent also holds among the objects of the relatum.[13] As such, analogies are based primarily on the assumption of structural similarities or isomorphisms: specifically, just as

---

[12] See George A. Miller, "Images and Models, Similes and Metaphors," in *Metaphor and Thought*, ed. Andrew Ortony, 2nd ed. (Cambridge, 1993), 357–400, esp. 368–81. A formal definition of an anology is given in Aristotle's *Poetics*: "I call 'by analogy' cases where *b* is to *a* as *d* is to *c*: one will then speak of *d* instead of *b* or *b* instead of *d*": Aristotle, *Poetics*, ed. and trans. Stephen Halliwell, Loeb Classical Library (Cambridge, MA and London, 1995), 1457b, lines 16–18 (104–5).

[13] See Dedre Gentner and Michael Jeziorski, "The Shift from Metaphor to Analogy in Western Science," in *Metaphor and Thought*, ed. Ortony, 447–80, esp. 448–50. See also Lawrence M. Zbikowski, *Conceptualizing Music: Cognitive Structure, Theory, and Analysis* (Oxford, 2002), esp. 3–19.

speech is composed of a finite number of indivisible and discrete elements, the letters, so can the sound of music be decomposed into indivisible and discrete elements known as notes (sounds, or *phthongi*). Not the same number and not the same sounds, to be sure, but the basic structure is the same. That is what is claimed in the elemental analogies.

But that is not the end of it. The second analogy from *Musica enchiriadis* goes beyond elemental structure and postulates the existence of "proper combinations" of the elements of music, just as correct language (Latin, in the event) is made up of "proper combinations" of letters into syllables, syllables into words, words into discourse, and so on. That is, not only are the basic structures of music and speech isomorphic; music, like speech, comes equipped with a combinatorial operator—the "rules" of the harmonic discipline—that dictates the primacy of certain intervals: the octave, the perfect fourth, and the perfect fifth. The example from Hucbald's *Musica* further extends the comparison by postulating a similarity between the actual physical material of human speech and musical sound: articulate sound in the first case and attuned or measurable sound in the second.

To be sure, the use of analogy is a very selective procedure in which certain structural properties or characteristics are postulated to be similar and are highlighted, and other properties or characteristics, possibly very significant ones, are simply ignored. But it is without doubt that these statements of similarity between speech and music, although selective, were extremely evocative, particularly, as I shall argue, to ninth-century Carolingian writers on the subject of music, who for various reasons were eager to accept and extend the authority of the Latin grammatical tradition.

Both the sound of speech and the sound of music are natural physical phenomena, which have, at least since Greek antiquity, been assiduously investigated. In the opening chapter of this study I establish the antique origins of the elemental model—the foundation of the postulated isomorphism—which was first applied to the sound of speech and then, by analogy, to the sound of music. I approach this examination through the work of the cognitive psychologist David R. Olson. In chapter 2, I consider the material analogy, a clarification of the "linguistification" of musical sound that proceeds from ancient Greek discussions of the nature of the physical material of the sound of speech and the sound of music. In the third chapter, I look at the origins of the combinatorial analogy and the historical connections between the theorization of speech and music. I argue in chapter 4 that during the Carolingian ninth century, the grammatical discipline, which had provided a structural model for musical sound, became a methodological paradigm for the study of liturgical music. This development, coupled with the Carolingian preoccupation with correct speaking and singing, led to the production of musical handbooks or treatises similar in style and procedure to grammatical handbooks or treatises. In my fifth chapter I present evidence indicating the similarity in function of musical notation to alphabetic writing in the textualization of classroom performance: notated musical examples were in fact intended to be read as text when embedded within transcribed theoretical discussion of liturgical music. I conclude my study with a brief discussion, within the context of the necessarily "selective" nature of the analogical process, of an important consideration that is not directly addressed in the traditional postulation of structural similarities between speech as base and music as target: does music have a semantic dimension, and if so, what sorts of conventions determine musical signification or meaning?

Chapter 1
The Elemental Analogy

In this chapter I investigate the origins of the elemental model that is the basis of the postulated isomorphism between the structure of human speech and the structure of musical sound, approaching this topic through a revisionist theory of the evolution of Greek alphabetic writing proposed by the cognitive psychologist David R. Olson.[1] Olson argues that writing in general has an epistemological function and that *alphabetic* writing, in particular, preceded the conceptualization of the sound of human speech — as letters ("phonemes"), syllables, words, and so on — and in fact provided the model by which the Greek language was introspected. I extend Olson's thesis and argue that this model, brought into consciousness by alphabetic writing, was also the basis, by process of analogy, for the ancient Greek introspection of musical sound that is evident in the writings of Plato and Aristotle and was codified in Greek music theory and transmitted to the Carolingian ninth century in the work of Calcidius, Martianus Capella, Boethius, and others. At the close of the chapter, I examine, within this context, Hucbald of Saint-Amand's comparison of two types of music notation, relating these two graphic systems for musical sound to considerations of the literal and illocutionary aspects of writing.

The "Alphabetic-Harmonic" Model for Musical Sound

I begin with a brief summary of the elements of Olson's revisionist history of writing which are relevant to the discussion at hand.[2] Two flawed assumptions must be put aside, Olson argues: the first, common since the time of Aristotle, that writing is a graphic device for transcribing speech; and the second, based on

---

[1] David R. Olson, *The World on Paper: The Conceptual and Cognitive Implications of Writing and Reading* (Cambridge, 1994; repr. 1996); henceforth Olson. An earlier version of some of the material in this chapter was originally published as B. Sullivan, "Alphabetic Writing and Hucbald's *Artificiales Notae*," in *Quellen und Studien zur Musiktheorie des Mittelalters*, vol. 3, ed. Michael Bernhard (Munich, 2001), 63–80.

[2] My summary is drawn primarily from Olson, chap. 4, "What Writing Represents: A Revisionist History of Writing," 65–90.

the first, that writing systems evolved in linear fashion from early pictorial systems to later phonological ones, culminating in the Greek alphabet, which was "uniquely successful in capturing the elementary constituents of the sound system of speech, namely, the phonemes of language."[3]

Olson maintains that the relation of writing to speech is just the opposite. Writing began as a form of communication, not as an attempt to transcribe speech; and the development of alphabetic writing around 750 B.C.E. was the fortuitous byproduct of an attempt to apply the Phoenician syllabary to the complex consonant and vowel system of the Greek language. Well-known arguments which assume that writing is a deliberate attempt to represent the sound patterns of speech suffer from what Olson calls a critical flaw: "They assume what they need to explain. Specifically, they assume that the inventors of writing systems *already knew* about language and its structure—words, syllables, phonemes, and the like—and that progress came from finding ways to represent those structures unambiguously."[4] On the contrary, Olson argues, "Awareness of linguistic structure is a product of a writing system, not a precondition for its development."[5] Writing systems represent speech, not in the conventional way, but by creating the very categories by which speech is brought into consciousness; writing is, in principle, metalinguistics: "We introspect our language along lines laid down by our scripts."[6] Simply put, for Olson, learning to read means learning to understand, and then hear, language in a certain way.[7]

Olson does reverse his ground somewhat by following his carefully argued presentation of what writing reveals about speech with a detailed analysis of what a specific writing system in fact ignores or even conceals—the "illocutionary"

---

[3] Olson, 65.

[4] Olson, 67. For earlier evolutionary accounts of the development of the alphabet, see, among others, David Diringer, *Writing* (London, 1962); and Ignace J. Gelb, *A Study of Writing*, 2nd ed. (Chicago, 1963).

[5] Olson, 68.

[6] Olson, 90. Olson makes a distinction between the cognitive resources involved in perception, which have evolutionary origins, and cognitive processes involved in the creation of artifacts which serve representational functions, which have cultural and historical origins.

[7] In support of this contention, see Richard M. Warren, *Auditory Perception: A New Analysis and Synthesis* (Cambridge, 1999), 170, who reports experimental evidence that illiterate adults are unable to segment speech phonetically. See also Robert J. Scholes and Brenda J. Willis, "Linguists, Literacy, and the Intensionality of Marshall McLuhan's Western Man," in *Literacy and Orality*, ed. David R. Olson and Nancy Torrance (Cambridge, 1991), 215–35. On the basis of experimentation with phoneme deletion, Scholes and Willis write (220): "The acquisition of the alphabetic representation of language enables the language knower to transfer this way of representation to speech. In short, we know about phonemes because we know about letters."

aspects of writing[8]—and I will return to this topic in due course. But first I would like to place and generalize Olson's theory within the Greek theoretical context. Alphabetic writing appeared around 750 B.C.E., and the cognitive model for the structure of human speech which it provided postulated a finite number of distinct sounds, considered to be "phonemes"—the vowels and consonants of the Greek alphabet—which in combination produced the complicated syllabic structure of the Greek language.[9] These syllables, in turn, combined into meaningful words, phrases, sentences, and texts, served to present an unambiguous "literal" record of what was said; and, following Olson's theory, alphabetic script, serving as a model for language and an object of study, allowed the formation of theories of grammar, that is, the detailed study of the components of speech and their proper combinations and usage. For example, Aristotle (384–322 B.C.E.) writes,

> The components of all diction are these: letter [element, *stoicheion*], syllable, connective, noun, verb, conjunction, inflection, statement. An element is an indivisible vocal sound (*phōnē*), but only one from which a compound sound is naturally formed: for animals too produce indivisible sounds, none of which do I term an "element."[10]

Aristotle's scheme for the systematic examination of human discourse is part of the Greek investigation of human speech which began in the fifth century with the philosophical studies carried out by the Sophists and continued through the work of Plato and Aristotle, the Stoics, the Roman grammarian Varro (116–27 B.C.E.), and late Latin grammarians such as Donatus and Diomedes.[11] But from

---

[8] See Olson, chap. 5, "What Writing Doesn't Represent: How Texts Are to Be Taken," 91–114.

[9] See Olson, "The History of the Alphabet," 78–90. Briefly, around 750 B.C.E., Semitic consonantal script was applied to non-Semitic Greek. Many of the syllable signs from the Semitic alphabet were used to represent Greek consonants. To allow for lexical contrasts made by vowel differences—present in Indo-European but not in Semitic languages—six Semitic characters were borrowed to represent isolated vowel sounds. "But equipped with such signs representing vowel sounds, the Greeks were in a position to 'hear,' perhaps for the first time, that those sounds also occurred within the syllables represented by the Semitic consonant signs. In this way syllables were dissolved into consonant-vowel pairings and the alphabet was born" (84–85). It is of course true that the individual letters of the Greek and Latin alphabets, contrary to classical and late Latin grammatical theory, were not phonemes; Warren (*Auditory Perception*, 169–72) argues that alphabetic symbols are more properly considered to represent articulatory gestures rather than sounds or hypothetical phonemes.

[10] Aristotle, *Poetics* 1456b, lines 19–24 (98–99). I will discuss this distinction between types of "compound" sound in chapter 3.

[11] For example, Varro writes: "Grammaticae initia ab elementis surgunt, elementa figurantur in litteras, litterae in syllabas coguntur, syllabis comprehenditur dictio,

the beginning this model for speech had a wider application. Certainly, the possibilities for ontological and epistemological generalization are evident in the fact that the Greek word customarily used for (sounded) "letter" was that for "element" (*stoicheion*) while the term for "combination" is "syllable" (*syllaba*). And, for example, in *Theaetetus*, Plato's dialogue on the nature of knowledge, Socrates examines the proposition that the acquisition of knowledge of any subject must begin with the identification of its primary indivisible elements; he uses as an example letters, the elements of writing, and their first combinations, syllables.[12] And Aristotle writes in *Metaphysics* that "that by which first we gain knowledge of a thing is the first measure of each class of objects," and gives as a specific example the indivisible sounds of the individual elements (vowels and consonants) of human speech.[13] That is, in these two examples, the generalized "element" defines the starting point of knowledge, just as the alphabetic letter is the indivisible starting point for the analysis of speech.

On a larger scale, one could argue that Plato's microcosmos is isomorphic to alphabetic-phonetic speech. In *Timaeus*, Plato's cosmological dialogue, Timaeus stresses the need to determine the essential nature of fire, water, air, and earth:

> For at present no one has as yet declared their generation, but we assume that men know what fire is, and each of these things, and we call them principles and presume that they are elements of the universe, although in truth they do not so much as deserve to be likened with any likelihood, by the man who has even a grain of sense, to the class of syllables.[14]

In these examples, the larger principle—whether ontological, cosmological, or epistemological—is derived from and justified by an appeal to the model provided by alphabetic writing.[15]

This model for the sound of human speech also had a more specific application. In *Theaetetus*, for example, Socrates moves from a discussion of learning

---

dictiones coguntur in partes orationis, partibus orationis consummatur oratio . . .": *Grammaticae Romanae Fragmenta*, ed. H. Funaioli (Stuttgart, 1969), 267. ["The first principles of grammar arise from the elements, which are formed in letters; letters are joined in syllables; syllables are united in utterance; utterances are joined in parts of speech; parts of speech are completed in speech . . ."]

[12] Plato, *Theaetetus*, trans. Harold North Fowler, Loeb Classical Library (Cambridge, MA, and London, 1921; repr. 1987), 201a–204c, esp. 202e (218–33).

[13] Aristotle, *Metaphysics Books I–IX*, trans. Hugh Tredennick, Loeb Classical Library (Cambridge, MA, and London, 1933; repr. 1996), 1016b, lines 18–24 (232–33).

[14] Plato, *Timaeus*, trans. R. G. Bury, Loeb Classical Library (Cambridge, MA, and London, 1929; repr. 1989), 48B–C (110–11).

[15] Plato offers a mythical explanation of the discovery of alphabetic writing by Theuth in *Phaedrus* 274C–275C. In *Philebus* 18B–C Theuth is credited with distinguishing and naming the letters which are the elements of speech.

to read as a process of distinguishing letters and syllables—the elements and elementary combinations of speech—to a discussion of studying music as a process of distinguishing notes (*phthoggos*)—the elements of musical sound.[16] And in *Philebus*, speaking of learning the sound (*phōnē*) of each letter of the alphabet, Socrates observes that "that which makes each of us a grammarian is the knowledge of the number and nature of sounds," adding that "it is this knowledge [of the number and nature of sounds] which makes the musician."[17] The *Sophist* presents the following exchange within the context of a discussion of dialectics:

> THE STRANGER: Now does everybody know which letters can join with which others: Or does he who is to join them properly have need of art?
>
> THEAETETUS: He has need of art.
>
> THE STRANGER: What art?
>
> THEAETETUS: The art of grammar.
>
> THE STRANGER: And is not the same true in connexion with high and low musical notes? Is not he who has the art to know the sounds which mingle and those which do not, musical, and he who does not know un-musical?
>
> THEAETETUS: Yes.[18]

So, not only did alphabetic-phonetic writing provide a model for speech (the so-called *stoicheion* model), which was generalized to a methodology for epistemological, metaphysical, and cosmological investigation; this model for the speech sounds of the human voice—based on division to a finite number of irreducible and distinct elements and recombination of these elements according to certain rules or principles of combination—was, in the Pythagorean-Platonic tradition, applied *by analogy* to musical sound.

This hypothetical isomorphism between speech and music, which I will call the "alphabetic-harmonic" model, is present in our early sources for Greek music theory. A complete statement, attributed to Adrastus (1st c. C.E.), is quoted by Theon of Smyrna (2nd c. C.E.). Note that Adrastus speaks of written as well as sounded speech:

> Just as the wholes constituting the primary parts of written sound and of all discourse are the verbs and nouns, and their parts are the syllables, which

---

[16] *Theaetetus* 206A–C (238–41).

[17] Plato, *Philebus*, trans. W. R. M. Lamb, Loeb Classical Library (Cambridge, MA, and London, 1925; repr. 1990), 17B–C (222–23).

[18] *Sophist* 253A–B (398–99).

themselves arise from letters, while the letters are the primary sounds, elementary, indivisible and smallest (for speech is put together out of letters as its first constituents and is resolved into them as its last), so also the wholes that are parts of melodic and attuned sound and of all melody are what are called *systēmata*: . . . they arise out of intervals [*diastēmata*], and the intervals out of notes [*phthongoi*], which once again are primary and indivisible and elementary sounds, out of which, as its first constituents, all melody is put together, and into which, as its last, it is resolved.[19]

Calcidius (fl. 4th or early 5th c. C.E.) includes this excerpt, revised and translated into Latin, in his commentary on Plato's *Timaeus*.[20] It is, in fact, a version of this Latin translation by Calcidius of the material from Theon of Smyrna which appears at the beginning of the Carolingian treatise *Musica enchiriadis*, quoted in my introduction.[21]

In *De musica*, Aristides Quintilianus (fl. 3rd c. C.E.?) writes that "a letter is the smallest part of articulate sound,"[22] with a parallel statement for musical

---

[19] Andrew Barker, ed., *Greek Musical Writings*, vol. 2, *Harmonic and Acoustic Theory* (Cambridge, 1989), 213–14. For the Greek text, see *Theonis Smyrnaei Philosophi Platonici Expositio Rerum Mathematicarum ad Legendum Platonem Utilium*, ed. Eduard Hiller (Leipzig, 1878; repr. New York and London, 1987), 49.6–20.

[20] *Timaeus a Calcidio Translatus Commentarioque Instructus*, ed. J. H. Waszink (London and Leiden, 1975), chap. 44 (92, lines 10–19); Calcidius ignores, however, the distinction between written and spoken sound that is present in the Greek text: "Just as nouns and verbs are the principal and greatest parts of articulate sound, which in turn are composed of syllables, which in turn are composed of letters, which are the basic, individual, and elementary sounds from which all speech is constituted and into which it can be decomposed, so are the principal parts of musical sound, which is called *emmeles* by the Greeks and is composed of modes and numbers, called intervals by musicians." The lemma to which this particular bit of commentary refers is taken from Calcidius's translation of *Timaeus* 36a–c (ed. Waszink, 28.7–9), the section in which the Demiurge constructs the soul of the world according to the principal ratios of the harmonic discipline. ["Etenim quem ad modum articulatae vocis principales sunt et maximae partes nomina et verba, horum autem syllabae, syllabarum litterae, quae sunt primae voces individuae atque elementariae—ex his enim totius orationis constituitur continentia et ad postremas easdem litteras dissolutio pervenit orationis—ita etiam canorae vocis, quae a Graecis emmeles dicitur et est modis numerisque composita, principales quidem partes sunt hae, quae a musicis appellantur systemata. Haec autem ipsa constant ex certo <con>tractu pronuntiationis quae dicuntur diastemata, diastematum porro ipsorum partes sunt pthongi, qui a nobis vocantur soni; hi autem soni prima sunt fundamenta cantus. Est autem in sonis differentia iuxta chordarum intentionem."]

[21] Schmid, 3, lines 1–5. For a comparison of Calcidius's text and the *Musica enchiriadis* text, see Phillips, "*Musica* and *Scolica enchiriadis*," 279–84.

[22] Barker, *Greek Musical Writings*, 2:445; *Aristides Quintilianus De Musica*, ed. R. P. Winnington-Ingram (Leipzig, 1963), 41; henceforth *Aristides Quintilianus De Musica*. For a discussion of Aristides's dates, see the Introduction to Thomas Mathiesen, *Aristides*

sound: "A note (*phthongos*) is the smallest part of melodic sound."[23] Greek alphabetic vocal notation, as transmitted in Alypius's *Institutio musica* (probably completed between the late fourth and the end of the fifth century C.E.), is, by its very nature, evidence of the primacy of the alphabetic model to the theoretical ordering of musical space.[24]

To summarize, I have argued that alphabetic writing served an epistemological function in the conceptualization by the Greeks of musical sound, as well as the sound of human speech. The resultant model for the "hearing" and "understanding" of musical sound postulates a finite number of distinct elements—the discrete harmonic pitches (*phthongoi*)—which were appropriate for melody and which could be combined into intervals, systems, and melodies, not according to the rules of intelligible human speech but according to the rules of the harmonic discipline. Plato's cosmology is in fact an intersection of the two models, for the ordering principle of the alphabetic microcosmos of the *Timaeus* is harmonic. Finally, just as the "literal" aspects of a text are the alphabetic-phonetic letters, sounded or written, the "literal" aspects of music are the discrete pitches, sounded or written.

In *De institutione musica* Boethius (ca. 480–524) transmits the principal components of the "alphabetic-harmonic" model for musical sound that he found in his Greek sources, including his adaptation of Alypius's exposition of Greek alphabetic musical notation.[25] For example, in *De institutione musica* 1.6 he writes, "Those things which are by nature unmixed are judged to be proper for harmony."[26] And *De institutione musica* 5.6, closely related to Ptolemy's *Harmonica* 1.4, reads in part, "Continuous pitches that are not in unison are not part of harmonic skill; they are dissimilar from each other but do not produce any

---

Quintilianus: On Music in Three Books (New Haven and London, 1983); he cannot be earlier than the first century C.E., and Mathiesen places him in the late third century.

[23] Barker, *Greek Musical Writings*, 2:406; *Aristides Quintilianus De Musica*, 7.

[24] Apparently Greek alphabetic vocal notation, using letters or modified letters of the Ionic alphabet, was developed by the fifth century B.C.E. Instrumental notation, using a combination of letters and symbols, was developed somewhat earlier. For a discussion of Alypius and his treatise, see Thomas J. Mathiesen, *Apollo's Lyre: Greek Music and Music Theory in Antiquity and the Middle Ages* (Lincoln, NE, and London, 1999), 593–607.

[25] For a discussion of Boethius's sources, see *Anicius Manlius Severinus Boethius, Fundamentals of Music*, intro., notes, and trans. Calvin M. Bower (New Haven, 1989), xxiv–xxix. On Boethius's use of Ptolemy, in particular, see Alan C. Bowen and William R. Bowen, "The Translator as Interpreter: Euclid's *Sectio canonis* and Ptolemy's *Harmonica* in the Latin Tradition," in *Music Discourse from Classical to Early Modern Times: Editing and Translating Texts*, ed. Maria Rika Maniates (Toronto, Buffalo, and London, 1990), 97–148.

[26] Boethius, *De institutione arithmetica libri duo, De institutione musica libri quinque*, ed. G. Friedlein (Leipzig, 1867), 193: "Ea namque probantur coaptatione consentanea, quae sunt natura simplicia."

one difference. Discrete pitches, however, are subject to the harmonic discipline; the difference between distinct pitches at an interval apart can be perceived."[27] Further, in the first sentence of *De institutione musica* 4.3, titled "On the names of the musical notes in Greek and Latin letters," he refers to the "necessarios sonos," that is, the finite number of discrete harmonic pitches of the three genera of the Greek gamut. And describing Greek musical notation, he makes an explicit analogy between alphabetic writing and alphabetic music notation, citing the benefits of a written record:

> They were also trying to make it possible for any musician wanting to write a melody over a verse . . . to adjoin the written signs (*notulae*) for the sounds. By means of this remarkable procedure they discovered that not only the words of songs, which are set forth by means of [alphabetic] letters, but also the melody itself, associated with these written signs, could endure in memory and in posterity.[28]

The important inference to draw from this statement of the analogy is that Boethius follows his Greek sources in accepting that the fundamentally constitutive—that is, "literal"—elements of a melody are the discrete harmonic pitches, just as the fundamentally constitutive "literal" elements of a text are the letters. The *notulae*, the signs for these pitches, establish the melody and allow it to be read and sounded in exactly the same way as the written letters establish the text and allow it to be read and spoken. Boethius's conceptualization of musical sound follows the alphabetic-harmonic model.

Hucbald of Saint-Amand's *Musica* draws heavily on Boethius's *De institutione musica*, and it is to that Carolingian treatise that I now turn to examine—principally within the context of what is now known as music notation—the impact

---

[27] *De institutione arithmetica*, ed. Friedlein, 357: "Continuae quidem non aequisonae voces ab armonica facultate separantur. Sunt enim sibi ipsis dissimiles nec unum aliquid personantes. Discretae vero voces armonicae subiciuntur arti. Potest enim distantium sibique dissimilium vocum differentia deprehendi . . ." Ptolemy had written that what is "proper to the sciences" is distinct and distinguishable and can be "encompassed by a definition or a ratio," as, for example, the sounds of the letters of the alphabet and the sounds of the notes of the harmonic discipline. Cf. Barker, *Greek Musical Writings*, 2:283–84; for the Greek text, see *Die Harmonielehre des Klaudios Ptolemaios*, ed. Ingemar Düring, Göteborgs Högskolas Årsskrift 36 (Göteborg, 1930), 9–10.

[28] *De institutione arithmetica*, ed. Friedlein, 309: ". . . ut, si quando melos aliquod musicus voluisset adscribere super versum rythmica metri compositione distentum, has sonorum notulas adscriberet, ita miro modo repperientes, ut non tantum carminum verba, quae litteris explicarentur, sed melos quoque ipsum, quod his notulis signaretur, in memoriam posteritatemque duraret." On Boethius's use of "notula," see Blair Sullivan, "*Nota* and *Notula*: Boethian Semantics and the Written Representation of Musical Sound in Carolingian Treatises," *Musica Disciplina* 47 (1993): 71–97.

of the "alphabetic-harmonic" model on an important Carolingian writer on *musica disciplina*.

Artificiales Notae and *Consuetudinariae Notae*

Boethius's footprints are evident in Hucbald's *Musica*,[29] but one thing in particular has changed since Boethius wrote: neumatic music notation has been invented and is in use in the Carolingian empire.[30] Hucbald bases his exposition of *musica disciplina* on the alphabetic-harmonic model; this intellectual position forces him, however, to attempt to resolve an inconsistency between two notational systems and the conceptualizations of musical sound they provide.

In his opening sentences Hucbald urges the student to learn the number and identity of the sounds which are the elements of melody and which are ordered and connected through the logic of numbers.[31] These *phthongi*, he writes, are the "most certain foundation of all song" ("certissima totius cantilenae fundamenta"), in other words, the literal elements of melody. That point is illustrated clearly as part of his presentation and adaption of Boethius's transmission of Greek pitch notation, which he calls "artificial" notation (*artificiales notae*). Paraphrasing Boethius's analogy, he writes that just as written letters allow a reader to determine what a text says *literally*, so do the written signs (*notae musicae*) for the *phthongi* allow someone trained in their use to sing the pitches or literal elements of a melody. He continues with a reference to neumatic musical notation: "This result [that is, being able to sing from sight] cannot be accomplished with the notation currently in use, which is composed of signs which vary from region to region, although it can serve as an aid to the memory."[32] This "customary" notation (*consuetudinariae notae*), as he calls it, is most emphatically not literal; in fact, it gives no information at all about the constitutive pitches of a melody:

---

[29] For a discussion of Hucbald's certain and likely sources, see Chartier, 51–59.

[30] Fundamental essays on the process of emergence of neumatic notation are reprinted in the following collections: Leo Treitler, *With Voice and Pen: Coming to Know Medieval Song and How It Was Made* (Oxford, 2003); and Kenneth Levy, *Gregorian Chant and the Carolingians* (Princeton, 1998). For a theological interpretation of neumatic notation, see Nils Holger Petersen, "Carolingian Music, Ritual, and Theology," in *The Appearances of Medieval Rituals: The Play of Construction and Modification*, ed. idem, Mette Birkedal Bruun, Jeremy Llewellyn, and Eyolf Østrem (Turnhout, 2004), 13–48, esp. 27.

[31] Chartier, 136: "Post et praeterea, quot uel quibus sonis qui uice habentur elementorum, tota regatur cantilena . . . quomodo scilicet haec omnia, uel uis de quibus ea <disciplina> tractat consonantiarum, rationabilitate congruentissima disponantur numerorum atque ad eorundem sint exemplar uniuersa composita atque compacta."

[32] Chartier, 194: "Quod his notis quas nunc usus tradidit quaeque pro locorum varietate diversis nichilominus deformantur figuris, quamuis ad aliquid prosint rememorationis subsidium, minime potest contingere."

"[The neumatic signs] lead the viewer on an uncertain path";[33] and "it is not at all possible, unless one hears it from someone else, to know what [intervals] the composer intended."[34] But, in light of this, Hucbald goes on to make a rather surprising proposal: he suggests appending the literal pitch notation—the clarity and certainty of which he demonstrates and extols—to the uncertain and inconsistent "customary" notation, the neumes. This seems to reverse priorities: following Hucbald's argument thus far, the literal notation should certainly take precedence over the other. There were, of course, issues of practicality in play; Hucbald does imply that neumatic notation was widely in use. But I think the surface discussion belies a tension between the literal and what I will call the illocutionary aspects of music notation—more generally, what a written text says as opposed to what it means when performative aspects are also considered.

It is certainly clear that any writing system represents, and brings into consciousness, certain things at the expense of others.[35] For example, alphabetic-phonetic writing provides an excellent model for the literal transcription of a spoken text. Using this technology, we can successfully preserve and recreate what was said; we cannot, however, from the written text alone, recapture tone and context, two extremely important aspects of meaning. Indeed, any number of devices have been appended to alphabetic-phonetic writing with the purpose of including an illocutionary or performative dimension, probably the most relevant to this discussion being punctuation and prosodic accent marks. Malcolm Parkes, for example, argues that the period, comma, exclamation point, and question mark can all be seen as lexical and graphic means for representing speech acts; and, more generally, he argues that punctuation can have what he calls "deictic" qualities, that is, punctuation can prescribe a particular interpretation of a text by means of selective pointing.[36] Now, Hucbald says about the non-literal "usual" (neumatic) notation that, despite its inaccuracies with respect to pitch, it is not entirely superfluous. Unlike the literal "artificial" notation, it can indicate tempo, vocal quality, phrasing, and cadences[37]—all of which, of course, are aspects of performance and interpretation without which, as he writes, "authoritative (*rata*)

---

[33] Chartier, 194: "Incerto enim semper uidentem ducunt uestigio . . ."

[34] Chartier, 194: ". . . nisi auditu ab alio recipias, nullatenus, sicut a compositore statuta est, pernoscere potes."

[35] For a general discussion of these questions, see Olson, chap. 5, "What Writing Doesn't Represent: How Texts Are To Be Taken," 91–114.

[36] Malcolm Parkes, *Pause and Effect: An Introduction to the History of Punctuation in the West* (Berkeley and Los Angeles, 1993), 70.

[37] Chartier, 196: "Hae tamen consuetudinariae notae non omnino habentur non necessariae, quippe cum et ad tarditatem seu celeritatem cantilenae, et ubi tremulam sonus contineat uocem, uel qualiter ipsi soni iungantur in unum uel distinguantur ab inuicem, ubi quoque claudantur inferius uel superius pro ratione quarundam litterarum, quorum nihil omnino hae artificiales notae ualent ostendere, ad modum censentur proficuae."

song is not created (*texitur*)."[38] Thus, in Hucbald's opinion, neumatic notation is a graphic means for representing performative acts about which pitch notation yields no information, a view of neumatic notation, as compared to pitch notation, that is quite like what Parkes describes in comparing the function of punctuation to that of unadorned alphabetic writing.

Let me summarize my argument. All writing has a cognitive dimension. In particular, alphabetic-phonetic writing, developed around 750 B.C.E., presented a model for understanding human speech that was in turn applied by analogy, in the Pythagorean-Platonic tradition, to the representation of musical sound as a finite number of discrete and irreducible pitches—the literal components of music—which could be determined and combined according to the rules of the harmonic discipline. This alphabetic-harmonic model and the associated pitch notation was transmitted through Boethius to Hucbald at a time when another system, adiastematic neumatic notation, was in use. In response to this circumstance, Hucbald produces a fascinating comparison of the two technologies. His conceptualization of musical sound is based on the alphabetic-harmonic model in which the constitutive elements of a song are its component pitches; thus he devises a notational system based on that model, his *artificiales notae*.[39] But, as he says, he realizes that the literal pitch notation gives no information about significant aspects of performance and interpretation, so he proposes glossing the customary neumatic notation, which has performative and interpretive content, with his alphabetic notation—somewhat like glossing punctuation marks with alphabetic text—in order to produce "a complete and errorless indication of the truth."[40]

I close this chapter with a suggestion, by way of contrast, of the elemental conceptualization of musical sound that is evident in another Carolingian treatise, Aurelian of Réôme's *Musica disciplina*.[41] The opening chapters of this treatise include rather undigested material excerpted from Isidore, Boethius, and Cassiodorus. Aurelian does mention that all music consists of six consonances and fifteen notes, giving the corresponding names of the notes in a section taken

---

[38] Chartier, 196. The use of "texere" is interesting, as it carries a connotation of materiality, that is, a text (in this case, musical) as a material replica of a composition. On this, see Brian Stock, *Listening for the Text: On the Uses of the Past* (Philadelphia, 1996), 41–42.

[39] I have not mentioned specifically the other notational system proposed by Hucbald—based on written syllables and lines representing tones and semitones—as he clearly considers it to be subsidiary to the pitch notation discussed above. Interval measurement is, in fact, directly derivable from the absolute measurement provided by a ordered collection of pitches.

[40] Chartier, 196: " . . . perfecte ac sine ullo errore indaginem ueritatis . . ."

[41] As noted in the introduction, Barbara Haggh argues that the text of Aurelian's treatise was written between 843 and 856 and then revised between 856 and 861: Haggh, "Traktat *Musica disciplina* Aureliana Reomensis."

from Cassiodorus, *Institutiones* 2.5.8.[42] But he asserts that the element of his musical cosmos—analogous to the letter in grammar and the unit in arithmetic—is not an individual pitch but a specific melodic gesture, or formula, the "tonus" or mode, of which there are eight.[43] And mathematical exactitude is a secondary consideration, as he indicates in the opening chapter of his tonary, dismissing the questions of the curious reader by sending him "to the music" if he wishes to learn about proportions, intervals, and the certitude of numbers.[44] Throughout his tonary Aurelian conceptualizes a chanted text as a string of syllables—each having a certain timbral characteristic and duration—moving in time through a series of melodic inflections or accentuations. Specific consonant intervals—introduced and accompanied with plainchant examples in chapter 2 of *Musica disciplina* and examined in some detail in chapter 6 in material excerpted from Boethius—are rarely mentioned and no specific ordered arrangement of pitches is presented; his primary considerations clearly lie elsewhere. Aurelian's conceptualization of musical sound, I would like to suggest, is also suggested by an aspect of writing, but not the collection of vowels and consonants that are basic to the alphabetic-harmonic model. The language of chapter 19 on verse recitation formulas, as given in the Gushee edition based on the Valenciennes manuscript, is particularly revealing in the present context, as it contains several references to music notation.[45]

The very opening paragraph of chapter 19 suggests that Aurelian's conceptualization of musical sound is quite different from Hucbald's, as Aurelian recommends a type of "prelectio" or pre-reading; preparation of a text, is, of course, a process that is traditionally related to the placement of written signs for punctuation and for accentuation in a text, that is, the specification of proper vocal motion, prosody, for the oral performance of a text. Referring in the text to music

---

[42] *Aurelianus Reomensis: Musica Disciplina*, ed. Lawrence Gushee (Rome, 1975), chap. 6, 70–76.

[43] *Musica Disciplina*, ed. Gushee 78: "Est autem tonus minima pars musicae, regula tamen; sicut minima pars grammatice littera, minima pars arithmeticae unitas. Et quomodo litteris oratio, unitatibus catervus multiplicatus numerorum consurgit et regitur, eo modo et sonituum tonorumque linea omnis cantilena moderatur." This material also appears in the treatise known as *Musica Albini*; see *Scriptores ecclesiastici de musica sacra potissimum*, ed. Martin Gerbert, 3 vols. (St. Blaise, 1784; repr. Hildesheim, 1963), 1:26–27. For a discussion of the authorship of *Musica Albini*, see Hartmut Möller, "Zur Frage der musikgeschichtlichen Bedeutung der 'academia' am Hofe Karls des Grossen: Die *Musica Albini*," in *Akademie und Musik: Festschrift für Werner Braun zum 65. Geburtstag*, ed. W. Frobenius et al. (Saarbrücken, 1993), 269–88.

[44] *Musica Disciplina*, ed. Gushee, 86: "Ceterum qui plenitudinem huiusce vult nosse scientiae, ad musicam eum mittimus, et si in ipsa voluerit versari, ad consonantiam proportionum ac speculationem intervallorum necne ad certitudinem oculos vertat numerorum."

[45] *Musica Disciplina*, ed. Gushee, 118: ". . . provida inspectione aut perspicatione antea circumvallentur oculo."

notation, Aurelian uses phrases such as *figura notarum, figura sonoritatis, figura melodie,* and *forma notarum.* His use of *figura* in this context is quite significant, as Paul Saenger has established that by the Carolingian ninth century, and particularly in the circles associated with Sedulius Scottus and Remigius of Auxerre, the word *figura* had come to be directly related to the written page.[46] Sedulius, in fact, writes that *figura* means the contour of a certain [written] phrase, with respect to length or height.[47] Furthermore, according to Sedulius, all text is reducible into minimal units of meaning, *partes* (definable as *dictiones*), each having an associated *figura.*[48] I maintain that Aurelian's statement that the element, or minimal part, of musical sound is a melodic rule, or mode, is related conceptually to this formulation; the fact that Aurelian uses *figura* to denote the written configuration of these modal intonation formulas strengthens the case.[49] Throughout his chapter 19 Aurelian transcribes to the written page through the use of descriptive language the melodic contour, as well as the tone quality, of a sequence of sung syllables moving through musical space. In particular, the language of prosodic accents, which has seen only very restricted use in the previous chapters, makes a significant appearance.[50] Charles Atkinson argues, based on the description given in words of the Introit psalm-tone for the first mode, that Aurelian refers to specific melodic gestures when he uses the terms *circumflexio* or *circumvolutio* (an ascent and descent of three notes) and *acutus* or acute accent (an ascent of two notes); Atkinson concludes that "both the prosodic accents themselves, as well as the terms used to describe them, are a part of the conceptual matrix of ninth-century musical notation."[51] I certainly agree, but I am suggesting further that the conceptual matrix is itself constructed with reference to various aspects of alphabetic writing.

---

[46] See Paul Saenger, *Space between Words: The Origins of Silent Reading* (Stanford, 1997), 83–92, 113–14.

[47] Sedulius Scottus, *In Donati artem minorem,* ed. Bengt Löfstedt, Corpus Christianorum Continuatio Medievalis 40C (Turnhout, 1977), 14: "Figura a fingo verbo oritur. Ergo figura proprie dicitur limitatio quaedam membrorum seu formarum longitudine seu latitudine seu his omnibus consistens, dicta a fingendo, id est a componendo."

[48] Sedulius Scottus, *In Priscianum,* ed. Bengt Löfstedt, Corpus Christianorum Continuatio Medievalis 40C (Turnhout, 1977), 73–75.

[49] I cannot demonstrate directly that Aurelian had access to these ideas; my case is circumstantial. But Saenger shows that these ideas penetrated the work of Remigius of Auxerre, and Barbara Haggh has suggested a connection between Remigius and Aurelian: see Haggh, "Traktat *Musica disciplina* Aureliana Reomensis."

[50] Prior to chapter 19 (*Musica Disciplina,* ed. Gushee, 118), *acutus* occurs once; *accentus* three times; and *circumflexus* not at all.

[51] Charles Atkinson, "*De Accentibus Toni Oritur Nota Quae Dicitur Neuma*: Prosodic Accents, the Accent Theory, and the Paleofrankish Script," in *Essays on Medieval Music in Honor of David G. Hughes,* ed. Graeme M. Boone (Cambridge, MA, and London, 1995), 17–42, here 40–42.

I have argued that the alphabetic-harmonic model presented explicitly by Hucbald is an adaptation of a model suggested by alphabetic-phonetic writing. On the other hand, Aurelian's implicit model of a moving sequence of inflected syllables—in which exact measurability of discrete pitches is a secondary consideration—is certainly related to identification of the *figura* or written configuration of textual elements, as well as written attempts to control the illocutionary or non-literal aspects of a text, for example, punctuation and prosodic accents. Thus, different aspects of writing bring different aspects of music into consciousness, establishing different conceptual priorities upon which graphic systems for music notation are based. Once in place, these graphic systems tend to reinforce the models upon which they are based; they are, in a sense, difficult to "rethink," a generalization of David Olson's work on alphabetic writing that is supported in experimental research in the field of music cognition reported by John Sloboda and Margaret Jean Intons-Peterson, among others.

In *Elementa Harmonica* 38–39, Aristoxenus (375–300 B.C.E.) wrote that "comprehension of music comes from two things, perception and memory."[52] Cognitive psychologists add a third mediating mental process between perception and memory, namely auditory imagery, the mind's reconstruction of an auditory experience in the absence of direct sensory instigation.[53] John Sloboda cites experiments demonstrating that the process of categorical perception and imagery involved in identification of the phonemes of a language closely parallels the categorical perception and imagery involved in identification of musical notes, in a particular culture.[54] On the subject of the role of cognition in auditory imagery and perception, Margaret Jean Intons-Peterson cites experimental evidence supporting the hypothesis that the representation of an auditory image reflects a subject's cognitive interpretation of the image and what it signifies, in addition to purely perceptual aspects; in other words, to a significant extent what a subject has learned to expect affects what is "heard."[55] These results are certainly consistent with my application of David Olson's theory of the epistemological

---

[52] Barker, *Greek Musical Writings*, 2:155; *The Harmonics of Aristoxenus*, 129.

[53] Ulric Neisser, for example, writes, "If memory and perception are the two key branches of cognitive psychology, the study of imagery stands precisely at their intersection": U. Neisser, "Changing Conceptions of Imagery," in *The Function and Nature of Imagery*, ed. P. W. Sheehan (New York, 1972), 233–51, here 233.

[54] John A. Sloboda, *The Musical Mind: The Cognitive Psychology of Music* (Oxford, 1985; repr. 1999), 23–24.

[55] Margaret Jean Intons-Peterson, "Components of Auditory Imagery," in *Auditory Imagery*, ed. Daniel Reisberg (Hillsdale, NJ, 1992), 45–71, here 63, 65. See also her description of a "general systems model" for auditory imagery, in which she proposes that "imagery, perception, and cognition may not be defined distincively, separately, and uniquely, but, rather, may recruit the similar processes to different extents, depending on the circumstances" (67).

function of alphabetic writing to music notation, namely, that learning any system of music notation involves learning to hear music a certain way: music notation not only helps us to remember and preserve musical sound, but it can significantly change how we think about and perceive music.

Conclusion

In this chapter I have argued that the ultimate source of the elemental analogy between speech and music, as it appears in Carolingian treatises on the theory and practice of music, is in fact the alphabetic-phonetic system of writing that appeared around 750 B.C.E. Taking the work of David R. Olson as a starting point, I have shown how the cognitive model provided by alphabetic-phonetic writing was not only generalized to define a methodology for philosophical investigation; it was also extended by analogy to the particular problem of the analysis of musical sound. The postulated isomorphism between music and speech is predicated upon a finite number of discrete and distinguishable elements—letters and notes—and combinatory operators: the rules of grammar and harmony, respectively. Finally, I have taken as a ninth-century case study of the effects of this "alphabetic-harmonic" model on Hucbald's discussion of two types of music notation:

1. alphabetic notation, in which the distinct and discrete elements of musical space are are assigned alphabetic written symbols, just as written alphabetic letters represent their sounded counterparts; and

2. ninth-century adiastematic neumatic notation, clearly related to attempts (such as punctuation and the use of prosodic accent markings) to control the non-literal or illocutionary dimension of a written text.

As I discussed in the introduction, analogy, carefully applied, can extend knowledge by providing a reasonable working model on which to base investigation. The careful application, of course, refers to the selection of the properties are to be included in the analogy and those that are to be ignored in a systematic comparison between speech and music, in our case. In this chapter, I have examined models for musical sound based on the elemental structure of language. In chapter 3 I will examine in detail the combinatorial analogy—the comparison between proper combinations of letters into syllables, words, and discourse, and musical notes into intervals, scales, and melodies. In chapter 2, as background for the discussion of appropriate combinations of elements, I set out some observations on the postulated similarities (and dissimarilarities) between the physical substance of human speech and that of musical sound: the material analogy.

CHAPTER 2
THE MATERIAL ANALOGY

Isidore of Seville (ca. 560–636) begins his discussion of music in book 3 of *Etymologiae sive origines* as follows:

> Music is the practical knowledge of melody, consisting of sound and song; its name is derived from "Muses." The Muses were named *apo tu maso*, that is, from inquiring, because, as the ancients would have it, with the Muses' assistance they inquired into the power of songs and vocal melody. The sound of these, because it is perceived by the senses, flows by into the past and is impressed upon the memory. For this reason, poets have written that the Muses are the daughters of Jove and Memory. Unless these sounds are held in human memory, they pass away, for they cannot be written (*scribi non possunt*).[1]

The last sentence of Isidore's paragraph makes a neat transition through a reference to memory to the intriguing assertion about the quality of the physical material of musical sound: it, unlike the sound of human speech, cannot be "written." This phrase has been interpreted in various ways; undoubtedly the most significant for students of Western music history is that Isidore with this sentence provides evidence that neumatic music notation was not in use in early seventh-century Spain, and probably had not yet been invented at all.[2] I have argued

---

[1] *Isidori Hispalensis episcopi Etymologiarum libri XX*, ed. W. M. Lindsay (Oxford, 1911; repr. 1966), 3.15. ["Musica est peritia modulationis sono cantuque consistens. Et dicta Musica per derivationem a Musis. Musae autem appellatae *apo tu maso*, id est a quaerendo, quod per eas, sicut antiqui voluerunt, vis carminum et vocis modulatio quaereretur. Quarum sonus quia sensibilis res est, et praeterfluit in praeteritum tempus inprimiturque memoriae. Inde a poetis Iovis et Memoriae filias Musas esse confictum est. Nisi enim ab homine memoria teneantur soni, pereunt, quia scribi non possunt."]

[2] See J. Fontaine, *Isidore de Séville et la culture classique dans l'Espagne wisigothique*, 3 vols. (Paris, 1983), 1:420–21; he writes (421), "Ces mots ont une double importance. Ils attestent d'abord qu'en écrivant sa 'musique,' Isidore n'oublie pas sa pratique personnelle du chant, son expérience directe de l'art musical. De plus, ils paraissent montrer que l'homme le plus cultivé du royaume wisigothique ne connaissait plus la notation musicale traditionnelle des Grecs, et qu'il ne connaissait pas encore la notation 'neumatique' du Moyen Age." Fontaine (1:421 n. 2 and 3:1093–94) gives a brief survey of scholarly

elsewhere, however, that Isidore's puzzling phrase offers no evidence at all about the existence of Visigothic neumatic notation—nor, for that matter, about his knowledge of the Greek system of pitch notation transmitted by Alypius—but is simply additional evidence of Isidore's well-known heavy reliance on grammatical theory.[3] Isidore's opening paragraph, through the words "unless these sounds are held in human memory, they pass away," is a patchwork of textual borrowings from Augustine's *De musica* and *De ordine* and Cassiodorus's *Institutiones*. The final phrase, stating that musical sound cannot be written, is found in several fourth- and fifth-century Latin grammar treatises and was in my opinion excerpted by Isidore from Diomedes's *Ars grammatica*, or from a text directly in the Diomedes tradition. In the following pages, I present the texts which are the basis of my argument, and then place this entire discussion within the context of classical and late classical discussions of the quality of the physical material of musical sound and of the sound of human speech.[4]

---

opinions for and against the existence of neumatic notation in Spain before the ninth century and describes, for his own part, the phrase *scribi non possunt* as "la négation brutale" (3:1092), an interpretation supported by the complete absence of neumed sources which can be dated to an earlier period. Michel Huglo, in 1994, describes Isidore's phrase as a "curious justification, drawn from the traditional etymology, of the oral transmission of music" ("Les diagrammes d'harmonique interpolés dans les manuscrits hispaniques de la *musica Isidori*," *Scriptorium* 48 [1994]: 171–86). In 1998, Kenneth Levy writes, "Isidore of Seville can probably be taken at his word, ca. 600, in his introductory paragraph on music in his encyclopedia, that 'unless sounds are retained by memory they vanish, as they cannot be written down'" (K. Levy, *Gregorian Chant and the Carolingians* [Princeton, 1998], 216).

[3] Blair Sullivan, "The Unwritable Sound of Music: The Origins and Implication of Isidore's Memorial Metaphor," *Viator* 30 (1999): 1–21. On the importance of grammatical theory to Isidore of Seville, see Fontaine, *Isidore de Séville*, chap. 1, "Le rôle de la grammaire dans la culture isidorienne," 1:1–56. See also Mark Amsler, *Etymology and Grammatical Discourse in Late Antiquity and the Early Middle Ages* (Amsterdam, 1989).

[4] For the complete details of my argument that Isidore's reference to the unwritability of musical sound was excerpted from Diomedes's treatise, or a treatise in the Diomedes tradition, see Sullivan, "The Unwritable Sound of Music," 5–11.

Grammatical Concepts of Articulate Sound and Undifferentiated Sound

Latin grammarians of the fourth and fifth centuries C.E. often presented a brief explanation of the physical material of the sound of human speech before proceeding to the exposition of the basic elements of discourse, the letters.[5] For example, Donatus (ca. 310–ca. 380) opens his *Ars maior* as follows:

> Sound (*vox*) is air which has been struck and can be perceived by the sense of hearing, to the extent that it is present. Every sound is either articulate or undifferentiated. Articulate sound can be composed with letters; undifferentiated sound cannot be written. The letter is the smallest element of articulate sound.[6]

With remarkable concision, Donatus mentions a theoretical model for the production of sound (as a disturbance of the air which is transmitted to the ears) and makes a distinction between articulate and undifferentiated sound: articulate sound can be expressed in letters while undifferentiated sound cannot be written.

Donatus's paragraph certainly belongs to the tradition of a paragraph on sound attributed to the Roman grammarian Varro (116 B.C.E.–27 B.C.E.):

> According to the Stoics, sound (*vox*) is a subtle current of air, which can be perceived by the sense of hearing, to the extent that it is present. It results either from the pulsing of a light breath of air or the percussion of air which has been struck. Every sound is either articulate or undifferentiated. Articulate sound is rational, clearly pronounced in human speech. It is also called literate or writable because it can be composed with letters. Undifferentiated sound is irrational and unwritable, present in the natural sounds of the voices of animals, for example, a horse's whinny or a bull's lowing.[7]

---

[5] For information on the history of Greek and Latin grammar, see Louis Holtz, *Donat et la tradition de l'enseignement grammatical* (Paris, 1981), 3–11; and see 49–121 for a detailed description of the pedagogical orientation and structures of late Latin grammar treatises. For a discussion of the origins and development of grammatical theory, see Martin Irvine, *The Making of Textual Culture: 'Grammatica' and Literary Theory, 350–1100* (Cambridge, 1994); and Robert Kaster, *Guardians of Language* (Berkeley, 1988). See also Amsler, *Etymology and Grammatical Discourse*, particularly the chapter "Technical and Exegetical Grammar before Isidore," 57–132.

[6] Holtz, *Donat*, 603: "Vox est aer ictus, sensibilis auditu, quantum in ipso est. Omnis vox aut articulata est aut confusa. Articulata est, quae litteris conprehendi potest; confusa, quae scribi non potest. Littera est pars minima vocis articulatae."

[7] *Grammaticae Romanae Fragmenta*, ed. H. Funaioli (Stuttgart, 1969), 268: "Vox est, ut Stoicis videtur, spiritus tenuis auditu sensibilis, quantum in ipso est. Fit autem vel exilis aurae pulsu vel verberati aeris ictu. Omnis vox aut articulata est aut confusa.

Three other fourth-century grammarians, Probus Minor, Marius Victorinus, and Diomedes, present different, less economical versions of the Varronian text on sound; furthermore, each one of them includes a specific reference to the sound of music. Probus's *Instituta artium*, written during the first half of the fourth century, reads as follows:

> Voice or sound is struck or beaten air, which is audible to the extent that it is present, and has an extended resonance. Every voice or sound is either articulate or undifferentiated. Human speech is articulate and can be composed with letters, for example, "write, Cicero," "read, Vergil," etc. Undifferentiated sound is either animate or inanimate and cannot be expressed in letters. Horses' whinnying, dogs' snarling, wild beasts' roaring, snakes' hissing, birds' singing, etc., are all animate; on the other hand, the ringing of cymbals, the crack of the whip, the pounding of waves, the crash of debris, the sound of the flute, etc., are inanimate. Man's voice or sound is undifferentiated when it cannot be expressed in letters, for example, laughter or whistling, coughing, etc.[8]

Probus's explanation of sound contains the essential elements of the Varronian tradition and can, in fact, be viewed as a gloss of either Varro or Donatus. To clarify the concept of inarticulate or undifferentiated sound, Probus creates a subclassification of undifferentiated sound—animate or inanimate—and gives several specific examples of each. Interestingly, animate, undifferentiated sound includes not only the calls of various fauna, but also human laughter, coughing, and whistling. Inanimate, undifferentiated sound is produced by waves, whips, falling objects, and two types of musical instrument: cymbals and flutes. The

---

Articulata est rationalis hominum loquelis explanata. Eadem et litteralis vel scriptilis appellatur, quia litteris conprehendi potest. Confusa est inrationalis vel inscriptilis, simplici vocis sono animalium effecta, quae scribi non potest, ut est equi hinnitus, tauri mugitus." For a detailed discussion of the ancestry and significance of this passage, see J. Collart, *Varron grammairien latin* (Paris, 1954), 57–63. Note that the distillation of this passage which Donatus gives omits Varro's first possible explanation of the physical nature of sound as a pulsing and subtle current, as well as his two specific examples of undifferentiated, thus unwritable, sound: whinnying and lowing.

   [8] *Grammatici Latini* 4:47: "Vox sive sonus est aer ictus, id est percussus, sensibilis auditu, quantum in ipso est, hoc est quam diu resonat. Nunc omnis vox sive sonus aut articulata est aut confusa. Articulata est, qua homines locuntur et litteris conprehendi potest, ut puta 'scribe Cicero,' 'Vergili lege' et cetera talia. Confusa vero aut animalium aut inanimalium est, quae litteris conprehendi non potest. Animalium est ut puta equorum hinnitus, rabies canum, rugitus ferarum, serpentum sibilus, avium cantus et cetera talia; inanimalium autem est ut puta cymbalorum tinnitus, flagellorum strepitus, undarum pulsus, ruinae casus, fistulae auditus et cetera talia. Est et confusa vox sive sonus hominum, quae litteris conprehendi non potest, ut puta oris risus vel sibilatus, pectoris mugitus et cetera talia."

sound produced by cymbals and flutes, says Probus, is *confusa*, undifferentiated, and cannot be composed with the sounds of letters; nor for that matter can the nonverbal sounds produced by human beings, such as whistling and, implicitly, humming.

The fourth-century rhetorician and grammarian Marius Victorinus, an older contemporary of Donatus,[9] makes in his *Ars grammatica* a more explicit and significant reference to musical sound:

> Sound (*vox*) is air which has been struck and can be perceived by the sense of hearing, to the extent that it is present. . . . There are two types of sound, articulate and undifferentiated. Articulate voice is understandable and writable and therefore is called "clearly spoken" by many and "intelligible" by some. What do the Greeks call it? Articulate sound (*enarthron phonen*). How many species does it have? Two. What are they? Musical sound—the sound of a flute or a horn or any musical instrument—and the articulate sound which is in common usage. Undifferentiated sound emits no discrete sounds or tones, for example, a horse's whinnying, a snake's hissing, applause, harsh noises, and so forth.[10]

Victorinus's text clarifies and extends, with references to Greek authority, the material on sound presented by Donatus, as does Probus's. Victorinus, however, differs from Probus in that he classifies musical sound not as undifferentiated but as one of two species of articulate sound.

Finally, Diomedes, in the paragraph on sound found in his *Ars grammatica*,[11] adds to a literal transcription of the text attributed to Varro an equally explicit reference to musical sound:

> According to the Stoics, sound (*vox*) is a subtle current of air, which can be perceived by the sense of hearing, to the extent that it is present. It results either from the pulsing of a light breath of air or the percussion of air which has been struck. Every sound is either articulate or undifferentiated.

---

[9] Holtz, *Donat*, 16–17 discusses the links between Donatus and Victorinus, who, Holtz argues, was dead by 380.

[10] *Marii Victorini Ars grammatica*, ed. I. Mariotti (Florence, 1967), 66: "Vox est aer ictus auditu percipibilis, quantum in ipso est. . . . Vocis formae sunt duae, articulata et confusa. Articulata est quae audita intelligitur et scribitur et ideo a plerisque explanata, a nonnullis intelligibilis dicitur. Hanc Graeci quid appellant? *Enarthron phonen*. Huius autem species quot sunt? Duae. Quae? Nam aut musica est, quae tibiis vel tuba redditur aut quolibet organo, aut communis, qua promiscue omnes utuntur. Confusa autem est quae nihil aliud quam simplicem vocis sonum emittit, ut est equi hinnitus, anguis sibilus, plausus, stridor et cetera his similia."

[11] Holtz, *Donat*, 83, places Diomedes's treatise in the decade 360–370; Kaster, *Guardians of Language*, 270–72, places Diomedes's work sometime between the middle of the fourth century and the middle of the fifth century.

Articulate sound is rational, clearly pronounced in human speech. It is
called both literate and writable because it can be composed with letters.
Undifferentiated sound is irrational and unwritable, present in the natural
sounds of the voices of animals, for example, a horse's whinny or a bull's
lowing. Some have also placed in this category the melodic sound (*vox modulata*) of a flute or any musical instrument, although despite the fact that
this type of sound cannot be written (*scribi non potest*), it can nonetheless be
measurably differentiated.[12]

Marius Victorinus writes that musical sound is articulate, and Diomedes seems
to agree, admitting that sources say that it can be decomposed into discrete and
measurable units in the same way that human speech can be decomposed into
the discrete sounds of the individual letters. On the other hand, Diomedes agrees
with Probus that musical sound is properly classified as undifferentiated sound,
specifically because it cannot be composed with the sounds of individual letters
of the alphabet. But Diomedes's statement to that effect is more direct and un-
equivocal than Probus's: Musical sound (*vox modulata*), the sound of a musical
instrument, despite the fact that it can be "measurably differentiated," cannot be
written: *scribi non potest*.

In summary, sound (*vox*) is a traditional topic, found in late Latin grammatical treatises, in which the sound of human speech is described as articulate and
writable; typically the discussion of sound includes examples of undifferentiated
and unwritable sound. A subtradition which specifically mentions musical sound
is found in the fourth-century treatises of Probus, Marius Victorinus, and Diomedes. Marius Victorinus seems to classify human speech and musical sound as
disjunct subcategories of articulate sound, *enarthron phonen*, as "the Greeks say."
Probus writes that musical sound is not articulate and therefore cannot be composed from letters. Diomedes is somewhat unclear as to whether or not he holds
that musical sound is articulate, but he states unequivocally that it cannot be
written, meaning that it cannot be decomposed into the sounds of the individual
letters of the alphabet and then represented by the written signs for these sounds.
Simply put, according to Diomedes — and subsequently Isidore of Seville — musical sound cannot be embodied in a text.

Clearly, the three texts are not consistent in their descriptions of musical
sound: Probus's text seems to come from a tradition that is distinct from that of

---

[12] *Grammatici Latini* 1:420: "Vox est, ut Stoicis videtur, spiritus tenuis auditu sensibilis, quantum in ipso est. Fit autem vel exilis aurae pulsu vel verberati aeris ictu. Omnis
vox aut articulata est aut confusa. Articulata est rationalis hominum loquelis explanata.
Eadem et litteralis vel scriptilis appellatur, quia litteris conprehendi potest. Confusa est
inrationalis vel inscriptilis, simplici vocis sono animalium effecta, quae scribi non potest,
ut est equi hinnitus, tauri mugitus. Quidam etiam modulatam vocem addiderunt tibiae
vel organi, quae, quamquam scribi non potest, habet tamen modulatam aliquam distinc-
tionem."

the analogy between letters and notes discussed in chapter 1; Diomedes's meaning depends on an understanding of what exactly is meant by "articulate" sound; and Marius Victorinus's text—also dependent for interpretation on an understanding of what his Greek sources call *enarthron phonen*—seems to refine the analogy between alphabetic letters and musical notes. In order to understand better the reasons for this apparent inconsistency, I now propose to take my lead from Marius Victorinus and examine a selection of classical Greek sources to investigate the origins of the concepts of "articulate sound" and "writability" and their use in theoretical discussions of the nature of physical sound and, in particular, of musical sound and the sound of human speech.

Physical Characteristics of the Sound of Speech and of Musical Sound

I begin with a passage from *Theaetetus* in which Socrates discusses the elements of human speech, the letters. Socrates challenges Theaetetus to give an explanation of the letter "S" by specifying its elements. Theaetetus replies:

> How can one give any elements of an element? For really, Socrates, the "S" is a voiceless (*aphōnē*) letter, a mere noise (*psophos*) as of the tongue hissing; "B" again has neither voice nor noise, nor have most of the other letters; and so it is quite right to say that they have no explanation, seeing that the most distinct of them, the seven vowels, have only voice, but no explanation whatsoever.[13]

This text—a brief excerpt from Socrates's presentation of the argument that knowledge of any subject begins with the identification of the elemental components of that subject—illustrates a distinction in the Greek language between the words *phōnē* and *psophos*. Plato's use of these terms, however, in the context of classification of the letters of the Greek alphabet is far from clear: vowels are voiced; some consonants make only unvoiced noise; and others, the mutes, have neither voice nor noise. In *Philebus* 17b–c, a text I mentioned in chapter 1, Socrates refers to two types of sounds: the sounds of human speech that are the elements of grammar and the sounds that are the elements of the musical art. In both cases, Plato uses exactly the same word for sound, *phōnē*, claiming that both the sound of speech and that of music can be decomposed into discrete elements which are the starting point of grammatical and musical knowledge—letters and notes, respectively. The two species of *phōnē* are not physically identical, to be sure, but they have the same "elemental" structure.

---

[13] Plato, *Theaetetus* 203b (226–29).

As quoted in chapter 1, Aristotle writes in *Poetics* that an element of speech is an indivisible vocal sound (*phōnē*) from which a compound sound is "naturally" formed; animals produce indivisible sounds which are not elements.[14] That is, he makes a distinction between elements of animate sound in general and those particular elements of animate sound which are in fact elements of human speech, the sounds of the letters of the alphabet. He reaffirms this idea in *On the Soul*, as part of a general exposition of sound and hearing:

> Now voice (*phōnē*) is the kind of sound (*psophos*) belonging to something alive, for no inanimate thing has a voice, but is said to do so by way of a metaphor, as are the aulos, the lyra, and all other inanimate things that are capable of prolongation, melody, and articulation (*dialekton*).[15]

Aristotle places an additional restriction on the concept of *phōnē* in a subsequent passage:

> For not every sound (*psophos*) made by an animal is voice (*phōnē*), as we were saying (for one can also make a sound with the tongue, or as people do when they cough), but that which makes the impact must be both alive and accompanied by some act of imagination, for voice (*phōnē*) is a sound (*psophos*) that has meaning.[16]

He goes one step further in *On Interpretation*, a treatise the name of which is suggested by the idea that human speech, oral and written, "interprets" thought. In the section on nouns, he introduces the concept of unwritable sound (or noise):

> No sound is by nature a noun: it becomes one, becoming a symbol. Noises which cannot be written (*agrammatoi psophoi*) can have meaning—for instance, those noises made by brute beasts. But no noises of that kind are nouns.[17]

---

[14] Aristotle, *Poetics* 1456b, lines 19–24 (98–99). I will discuss the idea of "naturally" formed sound in chapter 3.

[15] Aristotle, *On the Soul*, Loeb Classical Library (Cambridge, MA, and London, 1936; repr. 1995), 420b.6–14 (116); the English translation is from Barker, *Greek Musical Writings*, 2:79. The Peripatetic *De Audibilibus* (from no later than the mid-3rd c. B.C.E.) uses the metaphor "clearly etched" to describe appropriate musical sound; see Barker, *Greek Musical Writings*, 2:102.

[16] Aristotle, *On the Soul* 420b.29–33 (118); Barker, *Greek Musical Writings*, 2:79.

[17] Aristotle, *On Interpretation*, ed. and trans. Harold P. Cooke, Loeb Classical Library (Cambridge, MA, and London, 1938; repr. 1996), 1.16a.26–30 (116–17).

In these excerpts, Aristotle argues that the particular sound (*phōnē*) of human speech is animate, meaningful, and writable (in the sense of scriptible).[18] The sound of musical instruments is inanimate and, by implication, *psophos* rather than *phōnē*.

As reported by Diogenes Laertius (3rd c. C.E.), the Stoic philosopher Diogenes of Babylon (2nd c. B.C.E.), in his grammatical treatise *Handbook on Speech and Language*, uses the word *phōnē* for both the sound of speech and the cry of an animal. He specifies, however, that man's voice is articulate (*enarthros*), while the voice of an animal is just a percussion of air brought about by natural impulse. In addition, human speech is writable sound, that is, sound that can be reduced to letters, the elements of human speech.[19] Thus in this Stoic treatise, we find the essential elements of the Roman grammarian Varro's discussion of sound, quoted above: human speech is articulate and writable. Musical sound, however, is not mentioned.

Writing specifically on the subject of musical sound, Aristoxenus (375–300 B.C.E.), an Aristotelian phenomenalist, uses *melos* as a general term for musical sound at the opening of his *Elementa harmonica*,[20] but then turns directly to the identification and discussion of the two types of vocal sound or *phōnē*: continuous and intervallic. The former is characteristic of human speech and the latter of melody or *melos*.[21] Breaking with the Pythagorean-Platonic tradition, Aristoxenus never refers to a note as the *element* of *melos*, writing that "a note is the incidence of the voice (*phōnē*) on one pitch (*tasis*)."[22] But he also ignores the Aristotelian distinction between *psophos* and *phōnē* with regard to the sound of musical instruments, as it is clear throughout his discussion that he is speaking of intervallic vocal as well as instrumental sound, using *phōnē* in both cases.

A clear and concise version of the traditional discussion of the physical quality of the sound of speech and of the sound of music is given in the statement attributed to Adrastus (1st c. C.E.) by Theon of Smyrna (2nd c. C.E.), which I cited in chapter 1. Carefully setting out the structural isomorphism between speech and music, Adrastus [Theon] makes a distinction between the physical quality of each type of sound. The general term he uses for sound is *phōnē*, but the material of human discourse (*logos*) is "writable sound" (*eggrammatos phōnē*), while that of music (*melos*) is "melodic and attuned sound" (*emmelou phōnē, hermosmenē*

---

[18] Cf. Irvine, *Making of Textual Culture*, 30–31, who writes: "Aristotle continued Plato's metalanguage and consolidated the tropes that made articulate speech and writing convertible terms" (30).

[19] Diogenes Laertius, *Lives of Eminent Philosophers*, trans. R. D. Hicks, Loeb Classical Library (Cambridge, MA, and London, 1925, repr. 2000), 2: 64–67.

[20] See Barker, *Greek Musical Writings*, 2:126 n. 1.

[21] Barker, *Greek Musical Writings*, 2:132–35; for the Greek text, see *The Harmonics of Aristoxenus*, ed. Henry Stewart Macran (Oxford, 1902), 101–6.

[22] Barker, *Greek Musical Writings*, 2:136; *The Harmonics of Aristoxenus*, 107.

phōnē).[23] This distinction between the quality of the two types of material sound is maintained in the commentary written by Porphyry (ca. 232–305) on Ptolemy's *Harmonics* (2nd c. C.E.), although Porphyry speaks of "writable sound" and "melody" (*melos*), rather than melodic sound.[24]

Aristides Quintilianus (fl. late 3rd c.) follows Aristoxenus in postulating the continuous character of speech and the discontinuous or intervallic structure of music.[25] But then, in the passage from *De musica* cited in chapter 1, he refers to a note as "the smallest part of melodic attuned sound."[26] His parallel statement for human discourse refers to the Stoic grammatical tradition: "A letter (*stoicheion*) is the smallest part of articulate sound (*phōnē*)."[27]

Let me summarize the textual evidence bearing on the conceptualization of the material of physical sound that I have assembled from the available Greek sources, in loosely chronological order:

1. Plato refers to a distinction between *psophos* and *phōnē*, but generally uses *phōnē* to refer both to the well-formed and differentiable sound of human speech, and to the well-formed and differentiable sound of music.

2. Aristotle writes that voice (*phōnē*) is the sound (*psophos*) made by something alive; but in addition, the *phōnē* of human speech is both writable and meaningful. The sound of a musical instrument is properly called *psophos* but not *phōnē*, even though it has melody (*melos*) and enunciation or differentiation (*dialektos*).

3. Aristoxenus, writing specifically on musical practice, breaks with Aristotle and classifies both the sounds of musical instruments and the sounds of human speech as *phōnē*. The sound of speech (*logos*), however, is continuous, while that of music (*melos*) is intervallic.

---

[23] *Theonis Smyrnaei Philosophi Platonici Expositio*, ed. Hiller, 49.6–20.

[24] *Porphyrios zur Harmonielehre des Ptolemaios*, ed. Ingemar Düring, Göteborgs Högskolas Årsskrift 38 (Göteborg, 1932), 86.25–27 and 81.19–22, respectively. The phrase "melodic sound" (*emmelous phōnēs*) is, on the other hand, found in the anonymous writings on music known as *Anonyma de Musica Scripta Bellermanniana* from the first few centuries C.E. (*Anonyma de Musica Scripta Bellermanniana*, ed. Dietmar Najock [Leipzig, 1975], 21 and 49).

[25] Actually, Aristides postulates three types of sound: continuous (human speech), intervallic (music), and intermediate (a combination of the other two); see Barker, *Greek Musical Writings*, 2:404. Pitch (*tasis*) is defined as "the indivisible movement of sound": *Greek Musical Writings* 2:405. For the Greek text, see *Aristides Quintilianus De Musica*, 7–11.

[26] Barker, *Greek Musical Writings*, 2:406; *Aristides Quintilianus De Musica*, 7.

[27] Barker, *Greek Musical Writings*, 2:445; *Aristides Quintilianus De Musica*, 41.

4. The Stoic philosopher Diogenes of Babylon—as reported by Diogenes Laertius—writes that *phōnē* is animate sound in general, but that the specific *phōnē* of human speech, opposed to that of the cries of animals, is both articulate and writable.

5. Adrastus make a careful distinction between the sound (*phōnē*) of human speech (*logos*) and the sound (*phōnē*) of music (*melos*): the former is writable sound, while the latter is melodic attuned sound.

6. Aristides Quintilianus agrees with Aristoxenus that the sound (*phone*) of human speech is continuous, while that of music is intervallic, but in addition gives the parallel formulation: a note (*phthoggon*) is the smallest part of attuned musical sound; a letter (*stoicheion*) is the smallest part of articulate sound.

Significantly for our discussion, the distinction in Greek between "writable sound" and "articulate sound," evident in this cursory overview, is ignored by Calcidius in his translation into Latin of Adrastus's Greek text: he translates Adrastus's "writable sound" as the Latin *vox articulata*, articulate sound, the elements of which are the letters. On the other hand, he carefully maintains Adrastus's distinction between the material stuff of the sound of speech and that of music, translating *emmelou phōnē* as *vox canora*, musical sound.[28] And in my opinion it is just this distinction between articulate sound and melodic sound that is at the basis of the apparent inconsistencies among Probus, Marius Victorinus, and Diomedes. Probus takes the terms "articulate" and "writable" to be synonymous; therefore any sound, whether animate or inanimate, which cannot be reduced to the individual elements of human speech—the letters, and their written representations—is not articulate or, as he writes, undifferentiated. He includes musical sound, which is not discussed, as a separate species of sound.

Marius Victorinus, using the Greek term *enarthron phōnēn*, specifies two types of articulate sound: speech and music; that is, musical sound is not a distinct species but a subspecies of articulate sound. The implication here is that "writability"—reducibility to the sounds of the letters of the alphabet and their written representations—defines a subspecies of articulate sound that contains human speech, but not music.

Diomedes's text is certainly the most sophisticated of the three and, in fact, is the most representative of the distinction found in the texts of Adrastus and Aristides Quintilianus between the physical material of human speech and that of music. In Diomedes's formulation, the physical material of human speech is called "articulate sound" (*vox articulata*). This material has the property of being meaningful and writable; that is, its elemental structure consists of individual

---

[28] See chapter 1.

letters. On the other hand, the physical material of music is called "melodic sound" (*vox modulata*); this material has the property of being measurable, and its elemental structure consists of individual notes or pitches.

Conclusion

These texts on the nature of the physical material of the sound of speech and the sound of music achieve a significant clarification and extension of the analogy between letters and notes. The structural analogy, based on an postulated isomorphism between the elemental composition of speech and music, is still intact, but now a clear distinction is made between the two types of differentiable physical sound that are similar in structure: the sound of human speech—articulate (= writable in letters) sound—and the sound of music—melodic (= measurable, attuned) sound—are disjunct subclassifications of physical sound. Clearly Hucbald was influenced by this tradition when he wrote, as cited in my introduction to this study, that musical sounds were not the "sounds of inanimate objects or the cries of irrational animals" but those that could be "measured and determined by calculable quantities and could be used for melody."[29]

To return to this chapter's starting point, Isidore of Seville was not referring to what we call "music notation" when he wrote that musical sound could not be written; and, in fact, we do not know whether he was aware of the Greek system of pitch notation. Boethius, on the other hand, certainly knew about Greek notation when in the early sixth century he undertook a translation into Latin of Aristotle's *On Interpretation* and subsequently wrote two commentaries on that text. In particular, translating *On Interpretation* 16a.27–30, the excerpt referred to above, Boethius renders *agrammatoi psophoi* as *inlitterati soni* and *phōnē semantike*—the sound of a noun—as *vox significativa*.[30] It is interesting to note that in his second commentary on this passage, he is careful to specify (following Aristotle):

> Therefore, because nouns have their meanings established by convention, while the meanings of the unwritable sounds (*inlitterati soni*) of wild beasts are established by nature, the sounds (*voces*) of the latter are not called nouns. In general we say of all sounds (*voces*) that some can be written *in letters* and others cannot; and furthermore of those which are either writable or not at all, some have meaning and others have none.[31]

---

[29] Chartier, 76–77.

[30] *Commentarii in Aristoteli Peri Hermeneias*, ed. C. Meiser, 2 vols. (Leipzig, 1877–1880), 1:4: "Secundum placitum vero, quoniam naturaliter nominum nihil est, sed quando fit nota. Nam designant et inlitterati soni (*agrammatoi psophoi*), ut ferarum, quorum nihil est nomen."

[31] *Commentarii in Aristoteli Peri Hermeneias*, 2.60: "Ergo quoniam nomina secundum placitum significativa sunt, ferarum vero inlitterati soni secundum naturam, idcirco

Isidore, less explicitly, was also referring to alphabetic letters, which he regarded as soundless communication and a form of external memory.[32] Mark Amsler writes that to Isidore letters were "*vox articulata* without voice,"[33] and in chapter 5 I will investigate the extent to which the elements of musical notation—specifically alphabetic pitch notation and ninth-century neumatic notation—were by analogy considered to be "*vox modulata* without voice." But first I turn to the third component of the basic analogy, the existence of "natural" or "proper" combinations of letters and, by analogy, musical notes.

---

harum voces esse nomina non dicuntur. Universaliter autem dicimus: omnium vocum aliae sunt quae inscribi litteris possunt, aliae quae non possunt, et rursus earum quae vel inscribuntur vel minime, aliae significant, aliae vero nihil."

[32] Cf. *Etymologiae*, book 1, ed. Lindsay, 13.

[33] Amsler, *Etymology and Grammatical Discourse*, 136.

CHAPTER 3
THE COMBINATORIAL ANALOGY

In one of our earliest extant records of the association between the grammatical and musical disciplines, the Platonic dialogue *Greater Hippias*, Socrates mentions the Sophist Hippias's expertise in letters and syllables, rhythms and harmonies; Hippias enthusiastically agrees: "Harmonies indeed, my good fellow, and letters!"[1] Writing several centuries later, Quintilian (ca. 35 C.E.–ca. 100 C.E.), praising the musical art, attests to this ancient connection:

> So far I have attempted merely to sound the praises of the noblest of arts without bringing it into connexion with the education of an orator. I will therefore pass by the fact that the art of letters and those of music were once united: indeed Archytas and Euenus held that the former was subordinate to the latter, while we know that the same instructors were employed for the teaching of both . . .[2]

In this chapter I look for evidence of this association in the ways in which human speech and musical sound were theorized with respect to the justification of certain privileged combinations of the elements of each. In the case of grammar, what were the proposed rationales for the combination of alphabetic letters into syllables and words? And what were the explanations offered for the apparently "pleasing" sounds of harmonic (or melodic) combinations of certain pairs of musical tones? If, as Quintilian says, the same instructors took charge of both disciplines, is it possible to find in early theoretical discussions a common basis for the combinatorial principles of both speech and music?

---

[1] Plato, *Greater Hippias*, trans. Harold North Fowler, Loeb Classical Library (Cambridge, MA, and London, 1939; repr. 1992), 285c–d (352–53).

[2] Marcus Fabius Quintilianus, *The Institutio Oratoria of Quintilian*, trans. H. E. Butler, 4 vols., Loeb Classical Library (Cambridge, MA, and London, 1920; repr. 1989), 1.10.17 (1:167–69): "Laudem adhuc dicere artis pulcherrimae videor, nondum eam tamen oratori coniungere. Transeamus igitur id quoque, quod grammatice quondam ac musice iunctae fuerunt; siquidem Archytas atque Euenus etiam subiectam grammaticen musicae putaverunt, et eosdem utriusque rei praeceptores fuisse . . ."

Mythological Foundations of Speech and Music

Each discipline had a foundational mythology—the myth of Theuth for speech and the myth of the Pythagorean hammers for music—although it is difficult to know how credible these stories were to Greek philosophers and scholars. Paul Veyne has discussed this question at length, writing that Greek mythology had a dual character: "For the philosopher, a myth was an allegory based on philosophical truth; for the historians, a myth was somewhat skewed historical truth."[3] He mentions Plato specifically:

> Let me say in passing that both versions are found in Plato . . .; occasionally Plato creates his own myths, which are approximations of the Idea, and at other times . . . he comes across Greek historical myths and submits them to the same type of criticism used by contemporary historians. To Plato, however, philosophical allegory, that half-truth, corresponded both to the participation of the physical in the truth of the Ideas, as well as to the impossibility of a rigorous science of the purely physical.[4]

The story of Theuth, given in the *Philebus* in the context of a discussion of the principles of the finite and the infinite, is Plato's mythical account of the discovery or invention of the elements of human speech:

> When someone, whether god or godlike man—there is an Egyptian story that his name was Theuth—observed that sound was infinite, he was the first to notice that the vowel sounds in that infinity were not one, but many, and again that there were other elements which were not vowels but did have a sonant (*phōnē*) quality, and that these also had a definite number; and he distinguished a third kind of letter which we now call mutes (*aphōna*). Then he divided the mutes until he distinguished each individual one, and he treated the vowels and semi-vowels in the same way, until he

---

[3] Paul Veyne, *Les Grecs ont-ils cru à leurs mythes?* (Paris, 1983), 75: "Pour le philosophe, le mythe était donc une allégorie des vérités philosophiques: pour les historiens, c'était une légere déformation des vérités historiques." On the subject of Greek mythology, see also Jean-Pierre Vernant, *Les origines de la pensée grecque*, 7th ed. (Paris, 1997).

[4] Veyne, *Les Grecs*, 75: "Soit dit en passant, l'une et l'autre versions se retrouvent chez Platon . . . ; tantôt Platon forge ses propres mythes, qui sont des approximations de l'Idée, et tantôt . . . il rencontre sur sa route quelques-uns des mythes historiques grecs et les soumet alors au même genre de critique que faisaient les historiens de son temps. Toutefois, chez Platon, l'allégorie philosophique, cette demi-vérité, correspondait à la fois à la participation du sensible à la vérité des Idées et, néanmoins, à l'impossibilité d'une science rigoureuse du sensible."

knew the number of them and gave to each and all the name of letters . . .
He assigned to them all a single science and called it grammar.[5]

Note that in the Theuth legend letters are described in terms of their sonant
qualities: vowels are *phōnēenta* and consonants are *aphōna*; Plato describes a third
category, the semi-vowels, called *mesa*, which do not have the vocal quality of
vowels, but do have a certain sound.[6]

In the *Cratylus*, Plato discusses the "naming process," that is, the combination of these discovered elements of human speech into syllables and words by
a mythical "name-maker" whose purpose was to imitate the essential nature of
each thing by means of letters and syllables. After comparing this "imitative"
process to a painter's mixture of colors, Socrates admits, "It will, I imagine, seem
ridiculous that things are made manifest through imitation in letters and syllables; nevertheless it cannot be otherwise. For there is no better theory upon
which we can base the truth of the earliest names . . ."[7] So in Platonic mythology,
the elements of human speech are described in terms of their phonetic properties,
but are combined according to a nominative rationale.

Music's foundational mythology—the story of the Pythagorean hammers—is transmitted in book 7 of Nicomachus's (1st–2nd c. C.E.) *Enchiriadon*.
The problem that Nicomachus poses for Pythagoras is that of devising an instrument capable of measuring accurately the underlying numerical properties
of certain "pleasant-sounding" musical intervals, the perfect fourth, the perfect
fifth, and the octave:

> One day he [Pythagoras] was deep in thought and seriously considering
> whether it could be possible to devise some sort of instrumental aid for the
> ears which would be firm and unerring . . . While thus engaged he walked
> by a smithy and, by divine chance, heard the hammers beating out iron on
> the anvil and giving off, in combination, sounds which were most harmoni-
> ous (συμφωνοτάτους) with one another . . . He recognized in these sounds
> the consonances of the octave, the fifth, and the fourth . . . Elated, there-
> fore, he ran into the smithy and found by various experiments that the dif-
> ference of sound arose from the weight of the hammers . . .[8]

---

[5] Plato, *Philebus* 18b–c (226–27). In *Phaedrus* 274c–d Theuth is credited with the invention of numbers, arithmetic, geometry, astronomy, draughts, and dice, as well as letters.

[6] Cf. *Philebus* 17b–c. For a discussion of Plato's subclasses of letters, see Walter Belardi, *Filosofia grammatica e retorica nel pensiero antico* (Rome, 1985), 68–69.

[7] Plato, *Cratylus* 425c–d (142–43).

[8] *The Manual of Harmonics of Nicomachus the Pythagorean*, trans. and comm. Flora R.
Levin (Grand Rapids, MI, 1994), 83. For the Greek text, see *Musici Scriptores Graeci*, ed.
Karl Jan (Hildesheim, 1962), 245–46.

This story provides an excellent example of Veyne's "skewed historical truth," for it is certainly possible that the Pythagoreans discovered that on an instrument like a monochord sections of the string whose lengths are in the ratios 4:3, 3:2, and 2:1 vibrate in frequencies corresponding to the harmonic intervals of the fourth, the fifth, and the octave.[9] As is well known, however, and as Claudius Ptolemy determined in the second century C.E.,[10] the experimental results with hammers described by Nicomachus are not scientifically accurate; in fact, the pitch of sounds produced by hammers is not directly proportional to their weight. The assumption of this story, however, is that the simplicity and elegance of these numerical ratios, coupled with a conviction that the truths of mathematics are unchanging and eternal, account for the consonant status of their acoustical realizations. As Richard Crocker writes, "To the Pythagoreans, intervals are consonant because they sound consonant and because their ratios are simple."[11]

Whether viewed as philosophical metaphor or skewed historical truth, these mythical accounts of the foundations of human speech and music accomplish the transition from phenomenalist observation to *a priori* rationale. The hammer story begins with what is actually heard—certain pleasant or "consonant" frequencies, *not* weights or even string lengths—and identifies these musical sounds with *unheard* simple ratios of integers, the basic elements of Pythagorean mathematics. The legend of Theuth begins with the sound of human speech and presents a justification for hearing that sound in a certain way—namely, as composed of phonetic elements of three types[12]—while the "name-maker" story attempts to supply a non-phonetic rationale for the syllables and words of the Greek language. Both legends begin with observable phenomena—the composite sounds of speech and music—and move to theoretical non-observable explanations. This was, however, not the only approach, and I turn now to attempts to rationalize the composite sounds of speech and music on a observable basis by means of the related concepts of "sounding together" and "sounding as one."

---

[9] For a detailed discussion of Pythagorean numerology and theories of consonance, see Richard Crocker, "Pythagorean Mathematics and Music," *Journal of Aesthetics and Art Criticism* 22 (1963): 189–98. See also Zbikowski, *Conceptualizing Music*, 7–10. Andrew Barker, noting that "the familiar figure of Pythagoras, mystic, mathematician, philosopher and scientist, is almost entirely a construct of the Pythagorean revival of Roman times," discusses early attempts at the measurement of musical intervals: Andrew Barker, *The Science of Harmonics in Classical Greece* (Cambridge, 2007), chap. 1, "Beginnings and the Problem of Measurement," 19–30.

[10] For Ptolemy's comments on the suspension of weights as a means of measurement, see *Harmonics* 1.8, Barker, *Greek Musical Writings*, 2:291–93; for the Greek text, see *Die Harmonielehre des Klaudios Ptolemaios*, ed. Düring, 19–21.

[11] Crocker, "Pythagorean Mathematics and Music," 195.

[12] Note the relation of this story to David Olsen's linguistic theory summarized in chapter 1.

Composite Sound: "Sounding Together" or "Sounding as One"

The phonetic concept of alphabetic letters "sounding together" or "sounding in combination" appears in early discussions of combinations of letters. In the *Sophist*, for example, Plato addresses the question specifically in terms of sonant quality: there are proper and improper ways to join letters, as "some of these do not fit each other [literally, are not 'harmonic'], and others do." The vowels, the most sonant of the letters, "run through them all as a bond, so that without one of the vowels the other letters cannot be joined together."[13] According to Plato, it is precisely the sonant quality of vowels that makes syllabic combinations possible; consonants, which lack this quality, can be heard only in combination with vowels. These statements about letters are followed by a reference to proper combinations of musical notes, leading to a generalization of the combinatorial processes in various arts and branches of knowledge. Here Plato uses a very significant phonetic metaphor: in any discipline, it is necessary to know which elements are consonant (*symphōnē*) and which are not. He does not, however, use the term *symphony* with specific reference to the class of letters now known as "consonants," but only in a general metaphorical sense: when elements—musical or otherwise—are properly combined, they have a consonant—that is, "symphonic"—relationship.

Aristotle generally agrees with Plato's characterization of vowels and consonants, writing in the *Poetics* that an element of speech, a letter, is an "indivisible vocal sound" from which a "compound sound is naturally formed."[14] He follows Plato in calling vowels and consonants *phōnēenta* and *aphōna*, but introduces a different term for semivowels: *hemiphōna*. The consonant, he writes, produces no sound and becomes audible (acoustic) only in combination with the elements that do produce a sound:[15] "A syllable is a non-significant sound formed from the combination of a voiced element [vowel or semivowel] with a consonant."[16] He offers no justification, other than phonetic, for any particular combination of this type.

The related phonetic assertion that certain pairs of distinct musical tones, when sounded simultaneously, blend together to form a single tone—that is, "sound as one"—is an attempt to explain the physical sensation produced by "concordant" harmonic intervals; it also seems to have its roots in the works of Plato and Aristotle.[17] Plato, for example, suggests that concordant tones are

---

[13] *Sophist* 253a (398–99).

[14] *Metaphysics* 1456b.

[15] *Poetics* 1456b (98–99).

[16] *Poetics* 1456b.

[17] For additional references, see Barker, *Greek Musical Writings*, 2:409 n. 58. See also André Barbera, "The Consonant Eleventh and the Expansion of the Musical Tetractys:

somehow "similar" in motion, writing in *Timaeus* 80b, "By attaching a similarity, they blend together a single experience out of high-pitched and low-pitched movement."[18] And Aristotle writes, in a difficult passage from *On the Soul* 26b, that what is mixed and concordant (*symphōnē*) is *more pleasant* than either the high or low note alone.[19] In *On Sense and Sensible Objects* 447a, he explains that "it is easier to hear a tone by itself than when sounded with the octave, because they [the tones an octave apart] tend to obscure one another. This always happens with individual things out of which one whole is formed."[20]

The *Sectio canonis* (ca. 300 B.C.E, possibly by Euclid) continues this tradition with the following sentence: "Among notes we also recognize some as concordant (*symphōnía*), others as discordant, the concordant making a single blend (*krasis*) out of the two, while the discordant do not."[21] And several hundred years later Nicomachus writes in chapter 12 of the *Enchiridion*, "[Intervals] are concordant (*symphōnía*) when the notes which bound them . . ., when struck or sounded simultaneously, mingle with one another in such a way that the sound they produce is single in form, and becomes as it were one sound."[22]

Aristoxenian Phenomenalism

It is important to note that none of the cited physical descriptions of consonant tones "sounding as one" denies the existence of specific underlying mathematical properties of such tones. Even Aristotle, a phenomenalist, writes in *Posterior Analytics*: "What is concord? A ratio of numbers between a high-pitched sound and a low-pitched sound. Why does the high-pitched form a concord with the low-pitched? Because the high-pitched and the low-pitched stand in a ratio of numbers."[23] Aristotle's pupil Aristoxenus (4th c. B.C.E.), however, adopts a firm position against the invocation of abstract mathematical principles to justify

---

A Study of Ancient Pythagoreanism," *Journal of Music Theory* 28 (1984): 191–223, at 192–93. Barbera (193) observes that ". . . most ancient authors seem to associate the notion of consonance with a harmonic [simultaneous] rather than a melodic event."

[18] *Timaeus* 80b (212–15); Eng. trans. Barker, *Greek Musical Writings*, 2:62–63.

[19] *On the Soul* 26b (150–51), my emphasis.

[20] *On Sense and Sensible Objects* 447a (270–71).

[21] Barker, *Greek Musical Writings*, 2:193. For the Greek text, see Jan, *Musici Scriptores Graeci*, 149. Thomas J. Mathiesen, "An Annotated Translation of Euclid's *Division of a Monochord*," *Journal of Music Theory* 19 (1975): 236–58, at 254 n. 13, comments on the uses of *krasis* (a "homogeneous" blend) rather than *mixis* (mixture).

[22] Barker, *Greek Musical Writings*, 2:267. For the Greek text, see Jan, *Musici Scriptores Graeci*, 261–62.

[23] *Posterior Analytics* 90a, quoted from Barker, *Greek Musical Writings*, 2:70–71.

musical practice; referring to the Pythagoreans, among others, he writes in *Elementa Harmonica* 32:

> We try to give these matters demonstration which conforms to the appearances, not in the manner of our predecessors, some of whom used arguments quite extraneous to the subject, dismissing perception as inaccurate and inventing theoretical explanations, and saying that it is in ratios of numbers and relative speeds that the high and the low come about. Their accounts are altogether extraneous, and totally in conflict with the appearances.[24]

And in fact Aristoxenus scrupulously avoids such appeals to abstract principle, stating that the evidence of one's ears is the only determining factor in the identification of the basic concordant melodic intervals, the fourth, the fifth, and the octave. Focusing on proper melodic construction, that is, the successive, rather than simultaneous, combination of musical notes, he writes in *Elementa Harmonica* 18–19:

> But harmonically attuned melody [*to hērmosmenon melos*] must not only consist of intervals and notes: it demands also a way of putting them together which is of a special kind, and not haphazard, since it is plain that the property of being constituted out of intervals and notes is of wider scope, belonging also to that which is harmonically ill-attuned [*anharmoston*]. Since this is so, it must be granted that the most important factor, and the one carrying the greatest weight in the pursuit of the correct constitution of melody, is that which deals with *the process of combination* and its special peculiarities.[25]

Aristoxenus concludes that "this distinguishes musical melody from the other kinds: but it must be understood that this distinction has been drawn only in outline, since the details have not yet been explained."[26]

But, in fact, Aristoxenus—although stating clearly that the most important factor in the correct constitution of melody is the one dealing with the process of successive combination—never does provide a more detailed explanation of why certain intervallic combinations are "melodic-sounding" and appropriate, and others are not. He does, however, bolster his phenomenalist position with an ultimately extremely significant analogy. In *Elementa Harmonica* 27, echoing Aristotle's *Poetics* 1456b, he writes that there appears to be "a natural principle

---

[24] Barker, *Greek Musical Writings*, 2:149; *The Harmonics of Aristoxenus*, 123–24. See also Zbikowski, *Conceptualizing Music*, 10–11.

[25] Barker, *Greek Musical Writings*, 2:138, my emphasis. For the Greek text, see *The Harmonics of Aristoxenus*, 177–78.

[26] Barker, *Greek Musical Writings*, 2:138.

of combination" like that which governs the putting together of letters.[27] He re-states this idea in *Elementa Harmonica* 37, specifying that the determination of which successive combinations of musical tones are melodic and which are not is "similar to that concerned with the combination of letters in speech: from a giv-en set of letters a syllable is not generated in just any way, but in some ways and not in others."[28] In summary, Aristoxenus's resolutely phenomenalist argumen-tation with respect to the justification of melodic combinations rejects the prior authority of abstract mathematical principles but ultimately appeals to the prior, and apparently unquestionable, authority of the principles of the study of human speech, the grammatical discipline.

A Late Latin Synthesis

From the time of Aristoxenus until the end of the first century B.C.E., we have virtually no extant texts on the subject of musical theory. Theon of Smyrna, writ-ing in the second century C.E. in a work titled *Mathematics Useful for Reading Plato* (*Expositio rerum mathematicarum ad legendum Platonem utilium*), quotes ma-terial from Adrastus "the Peripatetic" (b. end of 1st c. C.E.), presumably so called because of his studies of Aristotle. In the first part of his treatise, as reported by Theon, Adrastus offers the analogy, cited in chapter 1, between letters as the elements of written and spoken sound and notes (*phthongoi*) as the elements of melodic and attuned sound. Several sections later, clearly echoing Aristoxenus, he appeals to grammatical authority to justify the existence of certain privileged melodic intervals:

> For as in speech and in written sound not every letter when joined to just any other produces a syllable or a word, so also in melody, in respect of at-tuned sound, not every note placed after just any other within the range of attuned sound makes a melodic interval, but only, as we have said, when placed according to certain determinate methods.[29]

In Theon's compilation, Adrastus, differing from Aristoxenus, continues with a discussion of these "methods," reporting that Pythagoras was the first to identify the ratios of concordant notes by means of experiments with lengths and thick-nesses of strings, weights attached to strings, and so on. Theon credits Adrastus with correctly documenting that a monochord, or *kanōn*, can be used to pro-duce these concordant intervals. He ends this discussion with an important

---

[27] Barker, *Greek Musical Writings*, 2:145; *The Harmonics of Aristoxenus*, 119.

[28] Barker, *Greek Musical Writings*, 2:153; *The Harmonics of Aristoxenus*, 128.

[29] Barker, *Greek Musical Writings*, 2:215. For the Greek text, see *Theonis Smyrnaei Expositio*, ed. Hiller, 52.17–22.

methodological statement that the experiment can be approached both empiri-cally and theoretically and the results will be the same: "[Adrastus] says that when these instruments designed for the discovery of the concords have been previous-ly prepared in accordance with the ratios, perception agrees with their testimony, while when perception has been taken first, reason is in attunement."[30]

On the subject of appropriate harmonic musical intervals Aristides Quin-tilianus (late 3rd c. C.E.), in book 1 chapter 6 of *On Music*, gives the traditional description of "sounding as one" or "sounding together":

> Again some notes are concordant (*symphōnē*) with one another, some dis-cordant (*diaphōnē*), some in unison (*homophōnē*). Concordant notes are such that when they are struck simultaneously, the melody is no more conspicu-ous in the higher than in the lower: discordant notes are those that when they are struck simultaneously the character of the melody properly belongs to one or the other.[31]

In chapters 20 and 21 of his treatise, now discussing the elements of articulate human speech, Aristides writes:

> Those elements which project a clear and fully audible sound are called vowels (*phōnēenta*), while those which come to the hearing indistinctly are called semivowels (*hemiphōnē*). Those which make a slight, faint sound are described as altogether 'mute' (*aphōnē*), as though this meant 'of little sound'.[32]

So far the terminology for vowels, semivowels, and consonants is exactly that of Aristotle; these subsets of the alphabetic letters are named on the basis of the quality of sound that they do or do not produce by themselves. But discussing combinations of letters, he writes,

> Combinations of elements produce syllables, which have the same names as the classes of vowel which they contain. Some take their values from a single element, others from several. Of these latter, some take their values from vowels . . . Others do so through consonants (*symphōnē*) too.[33]

This use of the word *symphōnē*—"sounding with" or "sounding together"—to refer to the letters of the alphabet formerly described as *aphōnē* or *hemiphōnē* in all likelihood began with the Alexandrian grammarian Dionysius Thrax (1st c.

---

[30] Barker, *Greek Musical Writings*, 2:220; *Theonis Smyrnaei Expositio*, ed. Hiller, 61.20–23.

[31] Barker, *Greek Musical Writings*, 2:409; *Aristides Quintilianus De Musica*, 9–10.

[32] Barker, *Greek Musical Writings*, 2:445–46; *Aristides Quintilianus De Musica*, 41.2–9.

[33] Barker, *Greek Musical Writings*, 2:446 (my emphasis); *Aristides Quintilianus De Musica*, 41.19–24.

B.C.E.), although the dating and authorship of the treatise attributed to him, the *Technè*, are uncertain.[34] In chapter 6 of the *Technè*, "On the Elements" (*stoicheion*), Dionysius identifies seven vowels, called *phōnēenta* "because they can produce a vocal sound by themselves"; and seventeen consonants, "called *sym-phōna* because although they cannot produce a vocal sound by themselves, in combination with vowels they produce a vocal sound."[35] But whatever the truth about its first use in grammatical theory, the use of *symphōna*, and its Latin translation *consonantes*, to describe the set of non-sonant letters is further evidence of the interrelationship of harmonic and grammatical theory.

I turn now to the treatise *De die natali*, an encyclopedic treatment of birthday mythology and lore by the third-century Roman grammarian and philosopher Censorinus; it provides a bifocal perspective on the classical-late Latin and the ninth-century Carolingian approaches to the question of the justification of consonant combinations. Composed in 238 C.E. for the forty-ninth birthday of Censorinus's patron, Q. Caerellius, this treatise is, by the author's admission, based on earlier commentaries, which undoubtedly included Varro's *Disciplinarum libri IX*, and probably the works of some one hundred other authors to whom he refers, among them Pythagoras, Plato, Aristotle, and Aristoxenus.[36]

Censorinus interrupts his general discussion of number, planetary motion, and the zodiac to summarize the particulars of what one "must know" about music in order to achieve complete understanding of his larger topic, temporal cyclicity:

---

[34] For a summary of the evidence, see Jean Lallot, ed., trans., and comm., *La grammaire de Denys le Thrace*, 2nd ed. (Paris, 2003), esp. 19–30. Lallot concludes that the evidence supports the assumption that at least the first ten chapters were written by Dionysius Thrax during the first century B.C.E.

[35] Lallot, *La grammaire de Denys le Thrace*, 44–45. Belardi (*Filosofia grammatica e retorica nel pensiero antico*, 71 n. 72) attributes the change in terminology to "the Stoics and Dionysius Thrax," although no extant Stoic treatises show that to be the case. Diogenes of Babylon, for example, in the summary of his teaching given by Diogenes Laertius, refers to twenty-four letters in the Greek alphabet, of which seven are vowels (*phōnēenta*) and six are mutes (*aphōna*); no intermediate classification is mentioned and the term *symphona* is not used in this context. See Diogenes Laertius, *Lives of Eminent Philosophers*, ed. Jeffrey Henderson, trans. R. D. Hicks, Loeb Classical Library (Cambridge, MA, and London, 1925; repr. 2000), 2:164–65.

[36] On Censorinus and the sources for and layout of *De die natali*, see Mathiesen, *Apollo's Lyre*, 612–18. Varro's treatment of grammar, dialectic, rhetoric, geometry, arithmetic, astronomy, music, medicine, and architecture has not survived; our knowledge of it is limited to several passages attributed to Varro by later writers. I will refer to Censorinus as the author of this brief text on music, although it may have originated with Varro; in either case, the discussion would be the same.

Music is the knowledge of proper melodizing (*scientia bene modulandi*). This melodizing occurs in sound (*vox*), but, in fact, some sounds have a sharper tone quality, while others are deeper in character. Individual unmixed musical sounds are called *phthongoi*. . . . Not all sounds are concordant in song when joined together in any way whatsoever. Just as our letters, if joined together at random, often will not fit together properly as syllables and words, so in music only certain intervals are able to produce symphonies. A symphony is a sweet singing together of two different notes joined to one another.[37]

Here Censorinus transmits the concept of "sounding together"; however, his discussion of music is the earliest extant Latin source for the definition of music as the "knowledge of proper melodizing," *scientia bene modulandi*, a definition which was subsequently taken up by Augustine, Martianus Capella, Cassiodorus, and Isidore of Seville, and eventually transmitted to the Carolingian ninth century.[38] As defined by Censorinus, proper melodizing, or melodic construction, is a process involving successive combinations of individual musical notes or *phthongi*, as the Greek word was transcribed in Latin. Following the Pythagorean-Platonic tradition, Censorinus treats the *phthongi* as the discrete and distinct elements of musical sound. The concept of proper melodizing, however, echoes Aristoxenus, and Censorinus follows exactly the Aristoxenian exposition of correct musical intervals, arguing by analogy with correct speech that only certain intervals are able to produce symphonies, and proceeding immediately to the Aristoxenian linear—as opposed to rational—definition of the principal symphonies or consonant combinations of notes: the fourth, two pitches separated by a distance of two whole tones and a half tone; the fifth, two pitches separated by a distance of three whole tones and a half tone; and the octave, two pitches separated by a distance of six whole tones.

But then Censorinus changes tack, abruptly dropping Aristoxenus's phenomenalist and non-rational approach to the justification of these privileged intervals; enter Pythagoras: "Now as it should be clear that musical sound could

---

[37] *Censorini de die natali liber ad Q. Caerellium*, ed. Nicholas Sallmann (Leipzig, 1983), 15–16: "Igitur musica est scientia bene modulandi. Haec autem est in voce, sed vox alias gravior mittitur, alias acutior. Singulae tamen voces simplices et utcumque emissae *phthoggoi* vocantur. . . . Sed non promiscue voces omnes cum aliis ut libet iunctae concordabiles in cantu reddunt effectus. Ut litterae nostrae, si inter se passim iungantur et non congruenter, saepe nec verbis nec syllabis copulandis concordabunt, sic in musica quaedam certa sunt intervalla, quae symphonias possint efficere. Est autem symphonia duarum vocum disparium inter se iunctarum dulcis concentus."

[38] See Augustine (354–430 C.E.), *De musica* 1.2; Martianus Capella (5th c. C.E.), *De nuptiis Philologiae et Mercurii* 9; Cassiodorus (ca. 490–ca. 585 C.E.), *Cassiodori senatoris Institutiones* (henceforth Cassiodorus, *Institutiones*) 2.5.2; and Isidore, *Etymologiae* 3.15, respectively.

not be measured by sight or by touch, I cite the invention of the admirable Pythagoras, who, *unlocking the secrets of nature*, discovered that the *phthongi*, the elements of music, correspond to certain numerical ratios."[39] Censorinus continues with a description of one of the acoustically flawed experiments described by Nicomachus, the means by which, according to this account, Pythagoras determined that the musical intervals of the fourth, the fifth, and the octave embody the simple and elegant mathematical ratios 4:3, 3:2, and 2:1, respectively.

Censorinus, although transmitting much of Aristoxenian theory, clearly wanted to ground the melodic and harmonic principles of the musical discipline in an authority able to bear the full weight of the more general theories expounded in his treatise, and appealing, as does Aristoxenus, to the existence of privileged combinations of letters and syllables is apparently not sufficient. That is, the grammatical analogy argues strongly for the existence of certain privileged melodic combinations; their exact determination, however, is another matter. Thus the move from physical evidence—the agreeable sound of these melodic intervals—to a priori principle—the elegant ratios which produce them—is accomplished by means of the foundational myth describing Pythagoras's fortunate and extraordinary access to eternal truth. In so doing, he presents a type of synthesis between phenomenalism based on the authority of the grammatical discipline and Pythagorean-Platonic idealism.

The Carolingian Context

The continuing authority of Pythagorean-Platonic harmonic theory is indicated by its transmission in discussions of the musical discipline subsequent to Censorinus's treatise. For example, the scientifically inaccurate myth of the Pythagorean hammers is presented in detail by Macrobius (fl. 430)[40] and mentioned by Cassiodorus (ca. 490–ca. 585),[41] who, after citing Censorinus, places Pythagorean-Platonic doctrine within a Christian framework:

> The musical discipline extends throughout all of the activities of our life: in the first place, if we follow with pure intentions the instructions of the Creator, we are following rules based on that discipline. In whatever we say, for example, we are moved within by pulsations of the arteries, which have been proven to be related through musical rhythms to harmonic moral

---

[39] *De die natali* 17 (italics are mine): "Nunc vero, ut liquido appareat, quemadmodum voces nec sub oculos nec sub tactum cadentes habere possint mensuras, admirabile Pythagorae referam commentum, qui *secreta naturae reserando* repperit phthongos musicorum convenire ad rationem numerorum."

[40] Macrobius, *Commentarius in somnium Scipionis* 2.1.

[41] Cassiodorus, *Institutiones* 2.5.1.

perfection. Music is the knowledge of proper melodizing. If we converse properly, we can be always associated with this discipline; when we act unfavorably, we are acting unmusically. Also, the things which are accomplished in heaven and earth through celestial direction would not be so without the musical discipline, for Pythagoras proved that this world was established by means of music and can be governed through it. This discipline also pervades the Christian religion . . .[42]

Boethius, following Nicomachus's version, gives the myth of the hammers a central position in his discussion of the inadequacy of physical evidence to determine the basic principles or rules of music, writing that Pythagoras abandoned the judgment of the senses and sought by rational means to determine complete and unchanging criteria for these consonances. The events having to do with Pythagoras's hearing the sounds of the hammers, and subsequently performing additional measurements with weights and tensions, led eventually, Boethius tells us, to the discovery of a "rule" (*regula*) and a means of accurate measurement of musical distances or intervals, the monochord.[43] And Isidore of Seville, drawing on Cassiodorus, mentions Pythagoras but greatly curtails Cassiodorus's Christian Pythagoreanism, keeping close to the subject at hand.[44]

Pythagorean mythology is not universally appealing, however, to Carolingian writers on the subject of music. Aurelian of Réôme includes the hammer story, writing somewhat dismissively that "the Greeks say that Pythagoras determined the scientific basis of the art [of music] from the sound of workmen's hammers," but that "Euclid and Ptolemy transmitted his teachings to posterity in a more satisfactory formulation."[45] And the myth of the hammers is not mentioned at all in Hucbald's *Musica* or in either of the *Enchiriadis* treatises, despite the importance of Boethius as a source for all three, and of Censorinus

---

[42] Cassiodorus, *Institutiones*, ed. R. A. B. Mynors (Oxford, 1937), 2.5.2–3 (143): "Musica ergo disciplina per omnes actus vitae nostrae hac ratione diffunditur; primum, si Creatoris mandata faciamus et puris mentibus statutis ab eo regulis serviamus. Quicquid enim loquimur vel intrinsecus venarum pulsibus commovemur, per musicos rithmos armoniae virtutibus probatur esse sociatum. Musica quippe est scientia bene modulandi; quod si nos bona conversatione tractemus, tali disciplinae probamur semper esse sociati. Quando vero iniquitates gerimus, musicam non habemus. Caelum quoque et terra vel omnia quae in eis dispensatione superna peraguntur, non sunt sine musica disciplina; nam Pythagoras hunc mundum per musicam conditum et gubernari posse testatur. In ipsa quoque religione valde permixta est . . ."

[43] Boethius, *De institutione musica* 1.10–11.

[44] Isidore of Seville, *Etymologiae* 3.16–17.

[45] Aurelian of Réôme, *Musica Disciplina*, ed. Gushee, chap. 2 (61): "Apud Grecos autem traditur Phitagoras ex malleorum fabrilium sonitu huius artis scientiam cognovisse atque aliis tradidisse, quem Euclides Ptolomeusque secuti studio clariore eius praecepta luculentius posteris tradidere."

as a source for *Musica enchiriadis* and *Scolica enchiriadis*.[46] In sections 7 through 11 of *Musica*, Hucbald presents the Aristoxenian "non-rational" definitions of musical intervals,[47] and then, in section 12, makes a careful distinction between "intervals" and "consonances," basing the identification of harmonic consonances entirely on the evidence of one's ears, that is, when two sounds are heard to combine into one tone.[48]

The omission of explicit references to Pythagorean mythology and abstract harmonic theory is particularly striking in chapter 10 of *Musica enchiriadis*, "On the symphonies," which begins with an almost literal quotation from Censorinus:

> Not all of the sounds described above join together equally sweetly nor are they concordant in song when joined together in any way whatsoever. Just as our letters, if joined together at random, often will not fit together properly as words or syllables, so in music only certain intervals are able to produce symphonies. A symphony is a sweet singing together of different notes joined to one another.[49]

A discussion of the three primary consonant intervals follows immediately, just as in Censorinus's treatise. But the issue of the justification of these intervals, other than by means of the evidence of one's ears and by analogy to the process of combining letters into syllables and words, is not raised.[50] The penultimate chapter of the treatise, however, closes with a reference to Christian Pythagorean-Platonic theory that is further developed in the concluding chapter: the fact that pleasant and agreeable sounds are produced by the mixture of certain tones, and not others, has a deep and hidden explanation, to which the Lord allows human access: the numerical principle that controls musical consonance.[51]

---

[46] On the influence of Boethius and Censorinus on the *Enchiriadis* treatises, see *Musica and Scolica Enchiriadis*, ed. and trans. Erickson, xli–xliv.

[47] Cf. Chartier, 142–47.

[48] Chartier, 148: "Consonantia siquidem est duorum sonorum, rata et concordabilis permixtio, quae non aliter constabit, nisi duobus altrinsecus editis sonis, in unam simul modulationem conueniant . . ."

[49] *Musica enchiriadis*, ed. Schmid, 23: "Praemissae voces non omnes aeque suauiter sibi miscentur nec quoquo modo iunctae concordabiles in cantu reddunt effectus. Ut litterae, si inter se passim iungantur, sepe nec verbis nec syllabis concordabunt copulandis, sic in musica quaedam certa sunt intervalla, quae symphonias possint efficere. Est autem symphonia vocum disparium inter se iunctarum dulcis concentus."

[50] This despite the availability of the complete Censorinus text: see Phillips, "*Musica and Scolica Enchiriadis*," 273–74.

[51] Cf. Schmid, 30–31. For a different interpretation of this material, see Calvin Bower, "'Adhuc ex parte et in enigmate cernimus . . .': Reflections on the Closing Chapters of *Musica enchiriadis*," in *Music in the Mirror: Reflections on the History of Music Theory and Literature for the 21st Century*, ed. Andreas Giger and Thomas J. Mathiesen (Lincoln, NE, and London, 2002), 21–44.

In part 2 of *Scolica enchiriadis*, entitled "About the Symphonies," the term symphony is first defined on empirical grounds: "an agreeable blending of certain musical tones."[52] Following an exposition of the basic consonances, the student asks for an explanation of why some notes are consonant and others are not; the reply is based on an analogy, but not a grammatical one, in this case: "Just as for counting consistently there is a simple system of numbering which is accessible even to children because of its ease — that is, 1, 2, 3, 4, etc. —. . . in the same way the *phthongi* in music, whose mother is arithmetic, that is, the numerical discipline, are determined in an easy way . . ."[53] The point is subsequently stated more succinctly: "As music is completely bound to the theory of numbers, as are the other mathematical disciplines [arithmetic, geometry, astronomy, music], we must understand these disciplines numerically."[54]

The purely mythological component of Pythagoreanism has all but vanished from these treatises. Pythagorean-Platonic harmonic theory, however, in its Christian reinterpretation, provides for these Carolingian writers what Nicholas Cook, following Carl Dalhaus, calls a "theological" epistemology:[55] the musical microcosm — the three perfect consonances, for example — is identified with the divinely-created natural macrocosm. The authority that was previously associated with Pythagorean-Platonic harmonic doctrine is now referred to the divine authority of the mathematical discipline. I believe that this development is best understood within the general context of what Michel Banniard has described as the "cultural genesis of Europe," the late antique process of preservation and transformation of the classical intellectual heritage, in which, by the eighth century, the grammatical discipline had expanded its traditional role to become a dynamic element in the adaptation and extension of classical knowledge, and the production of new texts.[56] No longer merely theoretically linked to the musical discipline by similar phonetic considerations, such as the concept of "sounding together," the grammatical discipline will provide to the Carolingians a paradigm for the study and practice of liturgical music.

---

[52] Schmid, 90: "Dulcis quarandam vocum commixtio."

[53] Schmid, 106: "Etenim sicut absolute computando simplex est series numerandi et facilitate sui etiam pueris patens, ut I II III IIII et cetera, . . . ita ptongi in musica, cuius mater est arithmetica, id est numeralis scientia, facili quidem ordine recensentur . . ."

[54] Schmid, 106–7: "Quae sicut per omnia numerorum rationi coniuncta est, atque ceterae mathesis disciplinae, ita per numeros oportet ut intellegantur."

[55] Nicholas Cook, "Epistemologies of Music Theory," in *The Cambridge History of Western Music Theory*, ed. Thomas Christensen (Cambridge, 2002), 78–105, at 80.

[56] See Michel Banniard, *Génese culturelle de l'Europe* (Paris, 1989).

CHAPTER 4
THE NINTH-CENTURY GRAMMATICAL PARADIGM

In *Institutio oratoria*, a lengthy treatise on the elements necessary to the education of an orator, Quintilian (1st c. C.E.) describes the grammatical discipline as consisting of "the knowledge of correct speech (*scientia recte loquendi*) and the interpretation of the poets."[1] This "knowledge of correct speech," a definition which Robert A. Kaster describes as "already centuries old" at the time of Quintilian, was conveyed as a "set of rules governing phonology, morphology, and the behavior of the individual parts of speech."[2] Simply put, according to Kaster, the grammarian had become the arbiter of correct speech, in general, and of proper word formation—the combination of letters and syllables—in particular.

The usage continues throughout late antiquity. For example, the grammarian Diomedes writes in the second half of the fourth century that "all of grammar consists principally in understanding the poets, the prose-writers, and the historians by means of a clear exposition, and of the principles of correct speech and writing."[3] Over one hundred years later Isidore of Seville in book 1 of *Etymologies* defines grammar to be "the knowledge of correct speech and the foundation of

---

[1] Marcus Fabius Quintilianus, *The Institutio Oratoria of Quintilian*, ed. G. P. Goold, trans. H. E. Butler, 4 vols., Loeb Classical Library (Cambridge, MA, and London, 1920; repr. 1989), 1.4.2 (1:62–63): "Haec igitur professio, cum brevissime in duas partes dividatur, recte loquendi scientiam et poetarum enarrationem . . ."

[2] Kaster, *Guardians of Language* 11–12. Kaster (11 n. 1) supports the contention that the tradition was already several centuries old with an excerpt from *Damascii Vitae Isidori reliquiae*. See also Michel Banniard, *Viva Voce: Communication écrite et communication orale du IVe au IXe siècle en Occident latin* (Paris, 1992), 342–45.

[3] Diomedes, *Ars grammatica*, Grammatici Latini 1:426–27: "Tota autem grammatica consistit praecipue intellectu poetarum et scriptorum et historiarum prompta expositione et in recte loquendi scribendique ratione." As I indicated in chapter 2, Holtz, *Donat*, 83, places Diomedes' treatise in the decade 360–370; Kaster, *Guardians of Language*, 270–72, places Diomedes' work sometime between the middle of the fourth century and the middle of the fifth century. See also, from the fourth century, Marius Victorinus, who describes the three branches of grammar as "intellectu poetarum et recte loquendi scribendique ratione" (Marius Victorinus, *Ars grammatica* 1.2 [65]); and Servius, who

liberal education."[4] At the beginning of book 2, "On rhetoric and dialectic," he repeats the definition, making a neat distinction between grammar and rhetoric: "In grammar we study correct speech; in rhetoric we study how to express what we have learned."[5]

But the simplicity of this statement of purpose and of Isidore's traditional distinction between grammar and rhetoric in no way indicates the influence and extent of grammatical methodology. Quintilian had, in fact, warned:

> Grammar, by which we mean the science of letters, must learn to know its own limits, especially as it has encroached so far beyond the boundaries to which its unpretentious name should restrict it and to which its earlier professors actually confined themselves. Springing from a tiny fountainhead, it has gathered strength from the historians and critics and has swollen to the dimensions of a brimming river, since, not content with the theory of speaking correctly, no inconsiderable subject, it has usurped the study of practically all of the highest departments of knowledge.[6]

Indeed, by the fourth and fifth centuries, Kaster writes, the grammarian, "controlling the access to eloquence with his texts in one hand and his cane in the other," was charged "to protect the language against corruption, to preserve its coherence, and to act as an agent of control."[7] In the words of Augustine, "Grammar is the guardian of articulate speech and a discipline which exercises control."[8] The grammarian, the purveyor of grammatical knowledge, presented himself as

---

writes, "Ars grammatica praecipue consistit in intellectu poetarum et in recte scribendi loquendique ratione" (Servius, *Explanatio in Donatum* 1, Grammatici Latini 4:486).

[4] *Etymologiae*, ed. Lindsay, 1.5: "Grammatica est scientia recte loquendi, et origo et fundamentum liberalium litterarum."

[5] *Etymologiae*, ed. Lindsay, 2.1: "In Grammatica enim *scientiam recte loquendi* discimus; in Rhetorica vero percipimus qualiter ea, quae didicimus, proferamus." It is interesting that Cassiodorus defines grammar as the "skill of speaking in fine style" ("peritia pulchre loquendi"), but does not fail to mention its regulatory role: "its function is correct composition of prose and metric texts" ("officium eius est sine vitio dictionem prosalem metricamque componere"): Cassiodorus, *Institutiones* 2.1 (94).

[6] Quintilianus, *Institutio oratoria* 2.1.4 (1:206–7): "Et grammatice (quam in Latinum transferentes litteraturam vocaverunt) fines suos norit, praesertim tantum ab hac appellationis suae paupertate, intra quam primi illi constitere, provecta; nam tenuis a fonte assumptis historicorum criticorumque viribus pleno iam satis alveo fluit, cum praeter rationem recte loquendi non parum alioqui copiosam prope omnium maximarum artium scientiam amplexa sit."

[7] Kaster, *Guardians of Language*, 17.

[8] Augustine, *Soliloquia* 2.11, PL 32.893: "Est autem grammatica vocis articulatae custos et moderatrix disciplina." The phrase originates with Seneca, *Epistle* 95.65. See Kaster, *Guardians of Language*, 17–18; and Banniard, *Viva Voce*, 343. See also Augustine, *De musica* 2.1, PL 32.1099: ". . . reprehendet grammaticus, custos ille videlicet historiae,

the arbiter of competing claims from three general areas: contemporary usage or convention (*consuetudo*), classical authority (*auctoritas*), and the natural properties of language (*natura*); thus Diomedes writes, citing Varro:

> Latinity is the attention to correct speech in compliance with the Roman language. As Varro states, this is based on four considerations: nature, reason (*analogia*), custom, and authority. The nature of verbs and nouns is immutable, transmitting to us neither more nor less than what it receives. . . . Reason is the process of putting in order the everyday language produced from nature, which, according to the experts, is simply the dissociation of foreign speech from learned speech just as silver is dissociated from lead. Custom is not produced by a rational process, but by men; therefore it is merely admitted, because it is validated by general agreement; and grammatical theory does not approve of it but nevertheless indulges it. . . . Authority is the most recent aspect of the rules of speech.[9]

The natural properties of language—the area in which questions about proper combinations of letters and syllables into words, phrases, and texts arise—were to be determined through systematic analysis (*ratio*) and put forth as rules (*regulae*) in a grammatical handbook, an *ars grammatica*.[10] The handbooks, then, in the absence of the grammarian himself would serve to answer any practical or theoretical questions which might arise under the general subject of "correct speech."

Furthermore, at least from the first century C.E. a knowledge of music was considered to be an essential element of a complete education, complementing the fundamental requisite, the ability to speak correctly. Quintilian, for example, discusses at length the advantages which a future public speaker might reasonably expect to derive from the study of music:

---

nihil aliud asserens cur hunc corripi oporteat, nisi quod hi qui ante nos fuerunt, et quorum libri exstant tractanturque a grammaticis, ea correpta, non producta usi fuerint."

[9] Diomedes, *Ars grammatica*, Grammatici Latini 1:439: "Latinitas est incorrupte loquendi observatio secundum Romanam linguam. Constat autem, ut adserit Varro, his quattuor, natura analogia consuetudine auctoritate. Natura verborum nominumque inmutabilis est nec quicquam aut minus aut plus tradidit nobis quam quod accepit. . . . Analogia sermonis a natura proditi ordinatio est secundum technicos neque aliter barbaram linguam ab erudita quam argentum a plumbo dissociat. Consuetudo non ratione analogiae sed viribus par est, ideo solum recepta, quod multorum consensione convaluit, ita tamen ut illi artis ratio non accedat sed indulgeat. . . . Auctoritas in regula loquendi novissima est."

[10] Cf. Kaster, *Guardians of Language*, 19. Kaster (183) describes the "natural" properties of language as difficult to define, although generally they are taken to be inherent in the grammarian's rules and give the grammarian a stable place to stand. "Correct usage," writes Kaster, "is assumed to be natural usage" (176).

Music has two modes of expression, in the voice and in the body [i.e., danc-
ing], for both voice and body require to be controlled by appropriate rules.
. . . Now I ask you whether it is not absolutely necessary for the orator to
be acquainted with all of these methods of expression which are concerned
first with gesture, second with the arrangements of words, and third with
the inflexions of the voice, of which a great variety are required in pleading.
Otherwise we must assume that structure and the euphonious combination
of sounds are necessary only for poetry, lyric, and so on, but superfluous in
pleading, or that unlike music, oratory has no interest in the variation and
arrangement of sound to suit the demands of the case.[11]

Quintilian's connection between correct and effective verbal expression and certain skills acquired through the study of music is maintained throughout late antiquity. Isidore, for example, echoes Quintilian's judgment about the importance
of musical knowledge by comparing its position in the classical curriculum to
that of letters: ". . . gradually this discipline was organized and enlarged in many
ways, and it was as much of a disgrace to be ignorant of music as to be ignorant
of letters."[12]

To summarize, by the end of late antiquity in the West grammar was en-
trenched as the discipline charged with making judgments about proper speech
and writing by means of rational investigations of the origins of language, the
use of authorities (principally Virgil), and the claims of convention or common
usage — often the source of incorrect speech. These judgments were made by the
purveyors of grammatical knowledge, the grammarians, and set out in handbooks, known generally as *artes grammaticae*. Throughout late antiquity, discussions of the musical discipline, although presenting a parallel definition of music as "proper melodizing" and emphasizing the equal importance of music and
grammar in the educative process, continued to appeal at least in part to the authority of the Pythagorean-Platonic harmonic tradition to justify basic precepts
of *musica disciplina*, in particular, the existence of certain privileged combinations
of musical tones. In the previous chapter I examined the emergence in Carolingian writings on music of pragmatic appeals to the authority of the grammatical
discipline and a growing disregard for Pythagorean mythology, as opposed to
traditional harmonic theory. I want now to examine that process in more detail,

---

[11] Quintilian, *Institutio oratoria* 1.10.22–23 (1:170–71): "Numeros musice duplices
habet in vocibus et in corpore, utriusque enim rei aptus quidam modus desideratur. . . .
Num igitur non haec omnia oratori necessaria? quorum unum ad gestum, alterum ad col-
locationem verborum, tertium ad flexus vocis, qui sunt in agendo quoque plurimi, per-
tinet: nisi forte in carminibus tantum et in canticis exigitur structura quaedam et inof-
fensa copulatio vocum, in agendo supervacua est; aut non compositio et sonus in oratione
quoque varie pro rerum modo adhibetur sicut in musice."

[12] Isidore, *Etymologiae* 3.16: ". . . paulatim directa est praecipue haec disciplina et
aucta multis modis, eratque tam turpe Musicam nescire quam litteras."

placing ninth-century Carolingian writing on the subject of music within a context in which *grammatica* had become not just a specific discipline but a methodology for investigation in all fields of knowledge.

Charlemagne and his counselor the Anglo-Saxon scholar Alcuin (ca. 732–804), who in 781 entered the imperial service, were faced with a sociolinguistic reality that Michel Banniard describes as the "Merovingian linguistic compromise" between educated speakers of Latin and uneducated listeners within previously Romanized regions.[13] This compromise consisted of a variety of localized usages of spoken Latin—"humble" or "rustic" speech—by means of which the Christian message had been effectively communicated throughout Merovingian territories. Eager to avoid scriptural misinterpretation, Alcuin—who regarded "linguistic anarchy" as a breeding ground for heretical error—determined to put in place a standard of correctness (*norma rectitudinis*) based on a return to the rules of Christian late antiquity in the areas of administration, liturgy, instruction, and language.[14] The nucleus of his plan was the reform of spoken and written Latin, so it is not surprising that Alcuin, in his brief treatise on the subject of grammar, seizes upon an element of the late Latin grammatical tradition that clearly stated the authority of the grammatical discipline. He writes, echoing Augustine and Diomedes: "Grammar is the knowledge of letters and the guardian of correct speech and writing; this knowledge is established by nature, reason, authority, and custom."[15] But Alcuin's belief in the importance of grammar went beyond the metaphor of the grammarian guarding the gates against intrusions of improper usage; he writes, syllogistically, in *De dialectica*:

> If it is valuable for a person to speak correctly, then grammar has value. There is, however, no doubt that correct speech should be valued. Thus grammar is valuable, because correct speech cannot exist without grammar. In the same

---

[13] See Banniard, *Genèse culturelle de l'Europe*, 202–3. See also idem, "Language and Communication in Carolingian Europe," in *The New Cambridge Medieval History*, vol. 2, *c.700–c.900*, ed. McKitterick, 695–708; R. Wright, "How Latin Came to Be a Foreign Language for All," in idem, *A Sociophilological Study of Late Latin* (Turnhout, 2002), 3–17.

[14] Banniard, in an extremely well-documented chapter, details Alcuin's Carolingian projects: *Viva Voce*, chap. 6, "Alcuin et les ambitions d'une restauration," 305–68; esp. 333.

[15] Alcuin, *Grammatica*, PL 101.857: "Grammatica est litteralis scientia, et est custos recte loquendi et scribendi; quae constat natura, ratione, auctoritate, consuetudine." Alcuin's *Grammatica*, which is found in three ninth-century manuscripts and commonly known as *Albini in Priscianum incipit liber primus*, is greatly dependent on Priscian's *Institutiones* (Priscian fl. 491–518); see J. R. O'Donnell, "Alcuin's Priscian," in *Latin Script and Letters A.D. 400–900: Festschrift Presented to Ludwig Bieler*, ed. J. J. O'Meara et al. (Leiden, 1976), 222–35.

way, if the absence of culture is undesirable, then studying grammatical treatises is desirable, for without grammar any man is uncultured.[16]

And not only was the study of grammar a prerequisite for the acquisition of
culture and knowledge; the circular letter generally known as *Epistola de litteris colendis*, sent ca. 784 by Charlemagne to all of his monasteries and bishops,
stresses that "those who desire to please God by living rightly should not neglect
to please him also by speaking correctly."[17] Indeed, as Martin Irvine describes it,
throughout this mandate "right living, right discourse, and right meaning (*recte
vivendo; recte loquendo, scribendo, legendo; rectus sensus*) are presented as intercon-
nected manifestations of living by rule."[18]

Musica disciplina, the study and practice of music inherited from antiquity
but now considered within a liturgical setting, was also an object of regulation,
because reforms in speaking and reading Latin had a direct application to chant
and psalmody. Indeed, *De litteris colendis* contains an admonition regarding correct performance of the holy office which establishes a direct parallel between
reading and chanting:

> For we desire you to be, as it is fitting that soldiers of the church should be,
> devout in mind, learned in discourse, chaste in conduct, and eloquent in
> speech, so that whosoever shall seek to see you out of reverence for God, or
> on account of your reputation for holy conduct, just as he is edified by your
> appearance, may also be instructed by your wisdom, which he has learned
> from your reading and singing, and may go away joyfully giving thanks to
> omnipotent God.[19]

---

[16] Alcuin, *De dialectica*, PL 101.965: "Si omni homini recte loqui bonum est, tum
grammatica bona est. Nulli dubium est, quin recte loqui bonum est. Utique grammatica
bona est, quia rectiloquium sine grammatica esse non potest. Item si rusticitas mala est,
utique grammaticam non legere malum est, quia omnis homo absque grammatica rusti-
cus est."

[17] Rosamond McKitterick, *Charlemagne: The Formation of a European Identity* (Cambridge, 2008), 316. McKitterick notes that only the copy sent to the monastery of Fulda
survives. The English translation is quoted from *Carolingian Civilization: A Reader*, ed.
Paul Dutton, 2nd ed. (Toronto, 2004), 90. See also Banniard, *Viva Voce*, 355; and Irvine,
The Making of Textual Culture, 307.

[18] Irvine, *The Making of Textual Culture*, 309.

[19] MGH *Capitularia regum Francorum*, ed. A. Boretius, vol. 1 (Hannover, 1883;
repr. 1984), 79, lines 38–42: "Optamus enim vos, sicut decet ecclesiae milites, et interius
devotos et exterius doctos castosque bene vivendo et scholasticos bene loquendo, ut, qui-
cunque vos propter nomen Domini et sanctae conversationis nobilitatem ad vivendum ex-
petierit, sicut de aspectu vestro aedificatur visus, ita quoque de sapientia vestra, quam in
legendo seu cantando perceperit, instructus omnipotenti Domino gratias agendo gaudens
redeat." Translation from *Carolingian Civilization*, ed. Dutton, 91.

In the Carolingian monastic and cathedral schools, the first major test of a student's progress in learning was mastery of the Psalter, and while learning to read the psalms the student also learned to sing them, thus obtaining the basic knowledge of chant necessary for the performance of the daily office, a routine task.[20]

Sometime before 819 Alcuin's former student at Tours, Hrabanus Maurus (ca. 780–856), in response to the urgings of his brothers at the monastery of Fulda who were preparing for priesthood, compiled from his classroom notes, written on individual pieces of parchment, the three-part encyclopedic handbook *De clericorum institutione* (*On Clerical Training*). Parts 1 and 2 introduce students to topics such as church hierarchy, the sacraments, and the liturgical year. Part 3 contains what Hrabanus describes as "the knowledge necessary to those in sacred orders," a brief exposition of the liberal arts curriculum. (Here, for intended clergy, he assumes mastery of the basics—reading, writing, calculation, and chant.) Within the liberal arts, Hrabanus gives pride of place to grammar (*grammatica*, the grammatical discipline, the "first liberal art"), defining it as "the knowledge of correct interpretation of poets and historians, and of correct speech and writing." Following Cassiodorus's *Institutiones*, one of his principal sources, he writes that this discipline is the "source and foundation of all of the liberal arts."[21] He continues, now quoting Augustine, "correct interpretation of scriptural allegory, enigma, and parable is not possible in the absence of grammatical knowledge."[22]

Hrabanus's discussion of music, the sixth liberal art, begins conventionally, quoting either Cassiodorus or Isidore: "Music is a discipline which speaks about numbers that are in certain proportions, namely, those proportions that are found in sound: duple, triple, quadruple, and so on, which are called proportions (*ad*

---

[20] John J. Contreni, "The Pursuit of Knowledge in Carolingian Europe," in *The Gentle Voices of Teachers: Aspects of Learning in the Carolingian Age*, ed. Richard E. Sullivan (Columbus, OH, 1995), 106–41, at 116. See also B. M. Olsen, "Music in Western Education in the Early Middle Ages," in *Ars Musica—Musica Sacra*, ed. D. Hiley (Tutzing, 2007), 29–40.

[21] Hrabanus Maurus, *De clericorum institutione*, ed. Detlev Zimpel, Freiburger Beiträge zur mittelalterlichen Geschichte 7 (Frankfurt am Main, 1996), 3.18 (468): "Grammatica est scientia interpretandi poetas atque historicos et recte scribendi loquendique. Ratio haec, et origo et fundamentum est artium liberalium." Cf. Cassiodorus, *Institutiones* 2, preface (91).

[22] Hrabanus, *De clericorum institutione* 3.18 (469): "Istorum autem troporum non solum exempla sicut omnium, sed quorundam etiam nomina in divinis libris leguntur, sicut allegoria, aenigma, parabola. Quorum omnium cognitio propterea scripturarum ambiguitatem dissolvendis est necessaria, quia <cum> sensus ad proprietatem verborum si accipiatur absurdus est quaerendum est utique, ne forte illo vel illo tropo dictum sit quod non intellegimus, et sic pleraque inventa sunt, quae latebant." Cf. Augustine, *De doctrina Christiana* 3.29.40–41.

aliquid).[23] But before continuing with material drawn directly from Cassiodorus, Hrabanus inserts the following sentences stating that just as knowledge of the grammatical discipline permits correctly spoken readings, musical knowledge is essential to the correct performance of the liturgy:

> This discipline is so noble and so useful that whoever lacks musical train-
> ing cannot properly perform the ecclesiastical office. Indeed, whatever is
> spoken properly in the readings and whatever is taken from the psalms and
> melodized sweetly in church is moderated by the knowledge of this disci-
> pline. And we not only read and psalmodize in church by means of it; we
> also perform all of our service to God in the required manner.[24]

Hrabanus continues with a word-for-word quotation of Cassiodorus's presentation of Christian Pythagoreanism,[25] but then leaves Cassiodorus's exposition of
the musical discipline—which proceeds with traditional material on the parts of
music, the types of instruments, the symphonies, and the Greek modes—and
concludes his discussion of music with a lengthy excerpt from Augustine's *De
doctrina Christiana*. The Augustinian material begins with a statement of the usefulness of music to an understanding of Scripture,[26] continues with examples of
biblical uses of number which admit musical interpretation, and closes with a justification of the search for knowledge in non-Christian sources: "A good and true
Christian realizes that wherever it may be found, truth belongs to the Lord."[27]

In assembling his notes, Hrabanus has carefully arranged an exposition of
the musical discipline which justifies its study on the basis of its role in moderat-
ing and enhancing the performance of the liturgical office (Hrabanus), its cosmic importance laid out in Christian Pythagorean terms (Cassiodorus), and its

---

[23] Hrabanus, *De clericorum institutione* 3.24(480): "Musica est disciplina quae de
numeris loquitur, qui ad aliquid sunt his, qui inveniuntur in sonis, ut duplum, triplum,
quadruplum, et his similia, quae dicuntur ad aliquid." Cf. Cassiodorus, *Institutiones* 2.21;
and Isidore, *Etymologiae* 2.24.15 and preface, bk. 3. Regarding the meaning of *ad aliquid*,
see Isidore, *Etymologiae* 3.6: "Per se numerus est, qui sine relatione aliqua dicitur, ut 3, 4,
5, 6, et ceteri similes. Ad aliquid numerus est, qui relative ad alios comparatur . . ."

[24] Hrabanus, *De clericorum institutione* 3.24 (480–81): "Haec ergo disciplina tam
nobilis est, tamque utilis, ut qui ea caruerit, ecclesiasticum officium congrue implere non
possit. Quicquid enim in lectionibus decenter pronuntiatur, ac quicquid de psalmis suaviter in ecclesia modulatur, huius disciplinae scientia ita temperatur, et non solum per
hanc legimus et psallimus in ecclesia, immo omne servitium dei rite implemus."

[25] Hrabanus, *De clericorum institutione* 2.24 (481).

[26] Hrabanus, *De clericorum institutione* 2.24 (481): "ac inde fit, ut non pauca etiam
claudat atque obtegat nonnullarum rerum musicarum ignorantia." Cf. Augustine, *De doctrina Christiana* 2.16.26.

[27] Hrabanus, *De clericorum institutione* 2.24 (483): "Immo vero quisquis bonus
verusque christianus est, domini sui esse intellegat, ubicumque invenerit veritatem." Cf.
Augustine, *De doctrina Christiana* 2.18.28.

usefulness in the decoding of difficult scriptural passages (Augustine). That is, Hrabanus's own contribution to this collage deals directly with correct and appropriate performance of the liturgical office, for which thorough knowledge of the grammatical discipline (*grammatica*) is fundamental but within which correct musical practice plays an indispensable role.

Hrabanus's brief collection of notes on the musical discipline is certainly not a guide to the technical aspects of liturgical music; it is a small piece of a large encyclopedic work and as such bears little resemblance to the detailed collections of rules for proper speaking and writing known as the *artes grammaticae*. But it is, on the basis of its explicit recognition of the centrality of the grammatical discipline and of the importance of musical knowledge to the performance of the liturgy, a significant step in the development of more substantial written discussions of music that show a unmistakable relationship to developments in ninth-century Carolingian writings on the subject of grammar.[28]

Vivien Law writes that Carolingian teachers had a fairly diverse collection of source materials from the late Latin grammarians available to them, but "no ancient grammar was appropriate as it stood for the needs of a late eighth- or ninth-century class. Carolingian teachers were as energetic as those of earlier generations in devising new solutions to old problems."[29] Carolingian scholars and teachers from Alcuin on were unwilling to abandon the authoritative material found in the late Latin grammatical texts by Donatus, Diomedes, Priscian, and others; but their needs and the needs of their students with respect to Latin pedagogy were different from those of the original audiences for these works, that is, native Latin speakers or advanced foreign students.[30] As Law documents, during the first half of the ninth century the principal Carolingian responses to this situation — which in addition to late Latin treatises from the fourth and fifth centuries drew upon insular elementary grammars developed during the seventh

---

[28] On various aspects of the relationship between ninth-century grammatical and music theory, see Bielitz, *Musik und Grammatik*; Bower, "The Grammatical Model of Musical Understanding in the Middle Ages"; Raymond Erickson's introduction to his translation of the *Enchiriadis* treatises, esp. xxxvi–xxxix; Nancy Phillips, "Classical and Late Latin Sources for Ninth-Century Treatises on Music," in *Music Theory and Its Sources: Antiquity and the Middle Ages*, ed. André Barbera (Notre Dame, 1990), 100–35; eadem, "*Musica* and *Scolica Enchiriadis*"; and William T. Flynn, *Medieval Music as Medieval Exegesis* (Lanham, MD, 1999), esp. chaps. 1 and 2.

[29] See Vivien Law, "The Study of Grammar," in *Carolingian Culture: Emulation and Innovation*, ed. Rosamond McKitterick (Cambridge, 1994) 88–110, at 92. Among the resources available from late antiquity, Law mentions Donatus's *Ars maior* and *Ars minor*; commentaries on Donatus by Servius, Sergius, Pompeius; Diomedes' *Ars grammatica*; and Priscian's *Institutiones grammaticae*.

[30] See Michel Banniard, "Latinophones, romanophones, germanophones: interactions identitaires et construction langagière (VIIIᵉ–Xᵉ siècle)," *Médiévales* 45 (2003): 25–42.

and eighth centuries—were pragmatic: the compilation of collections of extracts from authoritative writings often accompanied by glossaries and other forms of supplements; extensive use of the dialogue form as a pedagogical tool; and detailed commentaries—seldom officially "finished"—on texts such as Donatus and Priscian.[31] Classroom instruction was based on oral recitation, but students were asked to recopy authoritative extracts and other material for themselves, on to either wax tablets or parchment.

The methods used within the cathedral and monastic schools to recast and supplement grammatical treatises were also applied to authoritative texts on the subject of music for teachers and students whose immediate concerns now included the proper performance of the liturgy as well as the traditional topics. Hrabanus's cut-and-paste approach to his sources is an early example of the sort of ad hoc arrangement and supplementation, here applied to the musical discipline, that Law describes. At least by the middle of the ninth century teachers and writers on the subject of music had begun to compile autonomous texts or collections of notes and comments devoted entirely to musical theory and performance. In so doing, they cast themselves, either explicitly or implicitly, as the "guardians of music," now applying rational mediation to the competing claims of authority and custom in order to recognize and rectify incorrect liturgical practice within the diverse mixture of Gallican, Gelasian, and "Roman" or "Gregorian" usages.[32] To illustrate this point, and drawing on Law's discussion

---

[31] Law gives many specific examples of Carolingian treatises, but I cite as particularly relevant to my study the following: Alcuin, *Grammatica*, PL 101.849–902; Hrabanus Maurus, *Excerptio de Arte grammatica Prisciani*, PL 111.613–678; Remigius of Auxerre, *In artem primam Donati*, ed. W. Fox (Leipzig, 1902); and Sedulius Scottus, *In Donati artem minorem, In Priscianum, In Eutychem*, ed. Bengt Löfstedt, Corpus Christianorum Continuatio Mediaevalis 40C (Turnhout, 1977). On Carolingian methods of composition specifically within the musical discipline, see also J. Smits van Waesberghe, "La place exceptionnelle de l'Ars Musica dans le développement des sciences au siècle des carolingiens," *Révue grégorienne* 32 (1952): 81–104, esp. 89; Waesberghe mentions gloss, centonization, and compilation, but fails to make any connection with prior activity within the grammatical discipline.

[32] Nancy Phillips has written that the Carolingian writers on the subject of music were "essentially pragmatic in their approach; they largely chose from the late Latin sources what seemed to them to be pertinent to their own practice . . ."; she mentions the nature of the manuscript tradition as a possible explanation of this, but, in my opinion, misses an essential point in failing to note the relevance to Carolingian writers on music of prior and contemporary pragmatic responses to the central problem of teaching the Latin language. See Phillips, "Classical and Late Latin Sources," 134. On "Roman" and "Gregorian" usage, see Eric Palazzo's discussion of the "Gregorian" sacramentary, requested by Charlemagne from Hadrian I. What was sent was a papal sacramentary attributed to Gregory, so the Carolingian clergy had to supplement this, often using material from the Gelasian sacramentary in wide use under Pepin the Short. Pepin the Short

of Carolingian innovations and adaptations within the grammatical discipline, I consider briefly a transitional treatise, Aurelian's *Musica disciplina*, and two Carolingian examples of *artes musicae*, the anonymous *Musica enchiriadis* and its companion *Scolica enchiriadis*.

Aurelian's *Musica disciplina*, an autonomous work from around mid-century, opens with a statement of respect for the skills of the musicians of the past by comparison to contemporary singers, who may know a few rules but are not truly musicians.[33] A description of his essentially pragmatic mode of operation follows: "Through what I have been able to find here and there within the words of the musicians of the past and what I have heard from you and others, I have applied myself to writing this new work . . . ."[34] Thus he bases his treatise, which he describes as "a detailed discourse on the rules for melodic formations,"[35] on the authority of the past—which is in turn predicated upon the natural properties of music—through which he will arbitrate the claims of contemporary practice, that is, musical usage.

From the outset his plan closely resembles that of the Carolingian grammarian. Indeed, the first ten chapters of *Musica disciplina* draw heavily on the authoritative works of Augustine, Cassiodorus, Isidore, and Boethius, glossed frequently with scriptural passages, a procedure used widely by Carolingian grammarians to "Christianize" late-Latin treatises with their heavy reliance on examples from Virgil. Aurelian gives a specifically musical twist to this procedure by quoting

---

had requested a presbyterial sacramentary from Rome, and received the Gelasian, which was then supplemented with Gallican prayers, chants, and so on: Eric Palazzo, *Liturgie et société au Moyen Age* (Aubier, 2000), 199–202. On Merovingian and Carolingian liturgy in general, and on the nature of Carolingian "reforms" in particular, see Hen, *The Royal Patronage of Liturgy in Frankish Gaul*. Hen brilliantly puts to rest the "grand narrative" claiming that Charlemagne and his immediate successors intended to accomplish Romanization and uniformity of the liturgy of early medieval Francia. In Hen's words, "Diversity on top of an underlying unity is a more accurate way of describing the Frankish situation" (153). See also idem, "The Recycling of Liturgy under Pippin III and Charlemagne," in *Medieval Manuscripts in Transition: Tradition and Creative Recycling*, ed. Geert H. M. Claassens and Werner Verbeke (Leuven, 2006), 149–60.

[33] Aurelian of Réôme, *Musica Disciplina*, ed. Gushee, preface, 54: "Scio enim quia nobilissimi valde inveniuntur cantores. Huius autem fateor nisi vos solum me neminem artis vidisse peritum. Quidam et enim nostrorum multa musice norunt statuta, tamen ut fuerunt prisci nusquam, ut arbitror, invenitur musicus." Throughout this discussion, I accept Haggh's arguement that the text of Aurelian's treatise was written between 843 and 856 and then revised between 856 and 861; see Haagh, "Traktat *Musica disciplina* Aureliana Reomensis."

[34] *Musica Disciplina*, ed. Gushee, 54: "Ac per hoc quae sparsim in veterum dictis invenire potui sed et quae a vobis et ab aliis audivi, ipse novum opus condere studui . . . ."

[35] *Musica Disciplina*, ed. Gushee, 54: "regulis modulationum . . . rerum laciniosum praescriberem sermonem . . ."

liturgical music to illustrate the fundamental melodic ratios found in nature and transmitted by ancient authority. Thus, for example, he glosses "Pythagorean" material drawn from Boethius's *De institutione musica* (1.10) on the octave, the fourth, the fifth, and the whole tone with references to the introits "Inclina Domine aurem tuam," "Confessio et pulchritudo," "Circumdederunt me," and "Puer natus est nobis."[36]

In chapters 8 and 9 Aurelian identifies, describes, and names the "tones" or modes, the eight specific melodic gestures, or formulas, that are the "elements of liturgical music" and that control the formation of liturgical chant. His presentation, which makes use of a grammatical analogy,[37] follows the standard grammatical format in which the letters of the alphabet are introduced as the elements of speech, their properties are described, and their names and written symbols listed. The following nine chapters (chapters 10 through 18) are a detailed commentary on these eight elements of liturgical music, and together with chapters 8 and 9, form a tonary, a Carolingian innovation which classifies the liturgical chants according to "tone" or mode, using the Eastern terminology of the *oktoēchos*. Two earlier examples survive: the abridged St. Riquier tonary from the late eighth century (containing only five tones) and the tonary of Metz from around 830.[38] The "commentary" present in chapters 10 through 17 includes specific examples of the varieties found within each mode, along with the appropriate differences for the various antiphonal psalm tones; throughout, Aurelian applies the language of classic syllabic theory to the description of liturgical melody, a practice that I have discussed elsewhere.[39] I maintain that this Carolingian procedure of the classification and detailed description of liturgical chant was certainly inspired and reinforced by the exhaustive discussion of the eight parts of speech, and lists of conjugations and declensions added by contemporary

---

[36] *Musica Disciplina*, ed. Gushee, chap. 2 (62–63). Aurelian, however, mistakenly tries to associate these four intervals with the four authentic tones. It is interesting that these particular chants also gloss the same passage in several copies of Boethius's *De institutione musica*; see Phillips, "Classical and Late Latin Sources," 115–18. Interestingly, the ninth-century Irish grammarian Murethach, working and writing within the Carolingian empire, in two instances glosses material in his commentary on Donatus with citations of liturgical chant, the introit "Iubilate deo omnis terra" and the gradual "Laudate dominum de caelis"; see *Murethach in Donati artem maiorem*, ed. Louis Holtz, Corpus Christianorum Continuatio Mediaevalis 40 (Turnhout, 1977), 45 and 99, respectively.

[37] *Musica Disciplina*, ed. Gushee, chap. 8 (78): "Est autem tonus minima pars musicae, regula tamen; sicut minima pars grammatice littera, minima pars arithmeticae unitas. Et quomodo litteris oratio, unitatibus catervus multiplicatus numerorum consurgit et regitur, eo modo et sonituum tonorumque linea omnis cantilena moderatur."

[38] On the general subject of tonaries, see Michel Huglo, *Les Tonaires: Inventaire, Analyse, Comparaison* (Paris, 1971), esp. chap. 1, "Les Premiers Tonaires (VIIIe–IXe Siècle)," and chap. 2, "Le Tonaire des Anciens Théoriciens."

[39] See Sullivan, "Grammar and Harmony," 101–10.

grammarians to elucidate the bare-bones paradigms presented in the works of Donatus and Priscian, for example. Indeed, Aurelian argues by analogy from a total of eight parts of speech to a total of eight liturgical modes: "Just as no one can increase the eight parts of the grammatical discipline by adding more, so no one can increase the number of modes . . ."[40] The penultimate chapter makes an explicit connection between reading and singing with a statement that errors of performance can be avoided by a careful prior inspection of the music, analogous to the pre-reading (*prelectio*) of texts recommended to insure proper pronunciation and punctuation.

Throughout his treatise, Aurelian implicitly adopts the tone and manner of a guardian and adjudicator of proper melodizing, rather than simply that of an observer and describer of contemporary practice. I offer a few examples chosen from many:

> "It is not possible for any singer to doubt that the verses of the Offertories are introduced by means of these modes."[41]

> ". . . nevertheless because [a certain version] endured in former times, it must out of respect remain in current usage."[42]

> ". . . indeed, tenses must be joined to tenses, that is, present to present, and future to future; as in all literature, unless this is observed throughout the text, its refined intent will be disrupted by the strident sound of two things crashing into each other."[43]

---

[40] *Musica Disciplina*, ed. Gushee, chap. 8 (83): "Et sicuti quit nemo viii partes grammatice adimplere disciplinae ut ampliores addat partes, ita ne quisquam tonorum valet ampliare magnitudinem . . ." Huglo (*Les Tonaires*, 28) expresses surprise that the oldest tonaries classify by mode all liturgical chants, even those that involve no psalmody; he concludes that in the absence of any practical need for this, the authors of the tonaries must have been responding to theoretical or didactic needs. I would argue that they were in fact following a grammatical model that required the careful and complete classification of objects under consideration.

[41] *Musica Disciplina*, ed. Gushee, chap. 10 (87): "Quod versus offertoriarum per tonos in ipsis intromittantur, cantor nemo qui dubitet."

[42] *Musica Disciplina*, ed. Gushee, chap. 10 (89): ". . . tamen [quia] apud antiquos ita mansit, apud nos quoque ob eorum memoriam necesse est permanere."

[43] *Musica Disciplina*, ed. Gushee, chap. 15 (104): ". . . etenim tempora debent temporibus iungi, scilicet presens cum presenti, et futurum cum futuro; quod omnino in litteratura, nisi observetur, sensus humanus quasi quibusdam fragoribus concussus intercipitur."

"Although some say that these [antiphons] do not belong to this mode, they are nevertheless mistaken. Any accomplished singer of these tones can immediately make this distinction and this decision."[44]

"It is in this mode, O prudent singer, that many, not deviating but rather following an incorrect usage, lengthen short syllables and shorten long syllables . . ."[45]

Near the end of his final chapter, Aurelian reasserts the authority of his treatise: "We offer to singers this little book drawn from this art and these rules and set out in a proper order; they must, following the authoritative guidance given in what has been presented, reread and learn it. We declare that no one can achieve perfect melodizing in singing who has not applied himself to learning what is written above about this art."[46]

Aurelian's *Musica disciplina*, as an example of a developing genre, still contains long, relatively undigested excerpts from the encyclopedic works upon which much of the text is based; as such, it resembles Hrabanus's earlier effort. Its distinctive elements include its constant self-promotion as the last word on appropriate usage and the resolution of conflicts between custom and authority, as well as the ten-chapter elaboration of the eight church modes so reminiscent of contemporary supplements to grammatical texts. Aurelian's autonomous collection of notes on music is impressive compared to Hrabanus's brief discussion, more so on the basis of its technical detail about liturgical practice, however, than for its uncertain exposition of *musica disciplina*.

By the end of the ninth century, according to the work of Pierre Riché and John Contreni,[47] *musica disciplina* was taught everywhere that the liberal arts were taught; evidence of the increasingly sophisticated approach to the work of Boethius and Cassiodorus, for example, is the anonymous text *Scolica enchiriadis*. Its origins, and those of its frequent companion in the manuscript tradition *Musica enchiriadis*, are still unknown. Both treatises undoubtedly have complicated histories involving several stages of evolution possibly beginning in the first half of the ninth

---

[44] *Musica Disciplina*, ed. Gushee, chap. 16 (110): "Licet negent quidam has toni huius habere consonantiam, sed tamen falluntur. Hoc autem tonorum canti potens dinoscere ac diiudicare quam citius valet."

[45] *Musica Disciplina*, ed. Gushee, chap. 19 (127): "Est hoc in tono, o prudens cantor, quod plerique non devitantes, sed potius usu improbo consectantes, correptiones producunt et productiones corripiunt . . ."

[46] *Musica Disciplina*, ed. Gushee, chap. 20 (131): "Hac autem arte subnixum hisque regulis atque ordine compositum, hunc libellum cantoribus praebemus relegendum et cum auctoritate superius posita discendum, denunciantes nemini posse adesse perfectam cantandi modulationem qui non studuerit superius scriptam eiusdem artis habere notitiam."

[47] See Contreni, "The Pursuit of Knowledge," and Pierre Riché, *Écoles et enseignement dans le Haut Moyen Age, fin du Ve siècle–milieu du XIe siècle* (Paris, 2000).

century.[48] I think that a likely explanation of this is the way in which texts of this sort were actually used in monastic and cathedral classrooms. They frequently began, as in the case of Hrabanus Maurus, with a teacher's collection of separate notes that were at some point collated into a single document, momentarily at least "fixed" on parchment. But excerpts from this material were often copied by students only on wax tablets, and then possibly recopied in a different form on parchment. And teachers might add new material, as it became available. In other words, through the active participation of both teachers and students, the text continued to evolve, possibly in different ways in different locations. The text we know as the standard version of *Scolica enchiriadis*, probably from the end of the ninth century, can be described as an *ars musica*, by analogy to the Carolingian *ars grammatica*. It is written entirely in the relatively easily digestible question-and-answer form often used by Carolingian grammarians.[49] The treatise opens with a statement by the student (*discipulus*) of Censorinus's definition of music as the knowledge of proper melodizing.[50] The teacher (*magister*), however, wants to know more and responds by asking for a definition of proper melodizing; he is presented with a brief gloss on this concept. The gloss refers to both to the requisite pleasing sound (*melos suavisonum*) of appropriate melody and to the authority of the musical art (*quantum ad artem*);[51] apparently pleased with the student's answer, the teacher announces that together they will study the topics that are necessary to the knowledge of proper melodizing and to the avoidance of corruption of liturgical song, that is, the avoidance of incorrect usage.[52]

---

[48] For a discussion of the dating and authors of the two treatises, see Raymond Erickson's introduction to his translation of *Musica and Scolica Enchiriadis*, xxi–xxiv. Erickson observes that the structure of *Musica enchiriadis* is based on that of grammatical treatises currently in use by the Carolingians (xxiv–xxv, xxxvi–xxxix). I will not repeat the details of his excellent discussion here, but will simply note that we have in this treatise what can justifiably be called an *ars minor musicae*. The authoritative knowledge from the past has been smoothly incorporated into the underlying grammatical structure of the presentation, and the primary focus is now on the clear and concise laying-out of rules for the correct performance of liturgical music.

[49] Alcuin's influential treatise based on Priscian's *Institutiones grammaticae* is written as a dialogue between the *magister* and his two *discipuli*, a Frank and a Saxon; see Alcuin, *Grammatica*, PL 101.857–902.

[50] *Scolica enchiriadis*, ed. Schmid, part 1, 61: "M: Musica quid est? D: Bene modulandi scientia."

[51] Schmid, 61: "M: Bene modulari quid est? D: Melos suavisonum moderari. Sed haec quantum ad artem. Ceterum non bene modulari video, si quis in vanis suavitate artis abutitur, quemadmodum nec ipse, qui ubi oportet, arte uti non novit, quamvis quilibet devoto tantum corde Domino dulce canit."

[52] Schmid, 61: "M: . . . Quocirca cum ecclesiasticis canticis haec disciplina vel maxime necessaria sit, ne incuria vel imperitia deturpentur, videamus, quibus rebus opus sit ad bene modulandi facultatem."

The topics that follow are presented in "grammatical" order; here the elements of music are identified as mathematically determinable discrete pitches, not Aurelian's "melodic gestures." Everything is examined in great detail, with an emphasis on meticulous clarity and logical presentation. For example, the student asks why the teacher refers to four modes when in fact eight is the number that is usually given; and the teacher responds with a concise but detailed explanation of authentic and plagal modes, a distinction which is presented without explanation in *Musica enchiriadis*.[53] This sort of inquiry is facilitated by the dialogue form which permits an emphasis on the "why" of things, and demonstrates the influence of what Law has identified as an increased interest in and reliance on dialectic in Carolingian grammatical treatises in the second half of the ninth century: "Of the many Carolingian contributions to the study of grammar, that with the greatest theoretical implications was the revival of dialectic . . . . Where the grammarian was concerned with correct speech, the dialectician was anxious to use it accurately—to formulate precise definitions and logical arguments."[54]

The treatise has three sections: first, an *ars minor*, containing elementary topics relating to correct performance (*bene modulandi scientia*), such as properties of pitches, including their written symbols; the pitch-set; tetrachords; and common errors in singing. This is followed by a two-part *ars maior* devoted to more advanced material: first, a discussion of the symphonies, organal singing, and the important of mathematics to music; and next, a presentation of material on the harmonic, or natural, properties of music, drawn largely from Boethius and Cassiodorus, but now deftly incorporated into the dialogue form and brought to bear on contemporary musical practice. Pythagoras is not mentioned: in *Scolica enchiriadis*, the ultimate authority for musical knowledge is mathematics, that is, the study of the natural properties of numbers, analogous to the natural properties of language cited by the late Latin grammarians. *Scolica enchiriadis* is a fully-developed *ars musica* in which the music theorist—like the late Latin grammarian described by Kaster—acts as the guardian of proper liturgical melodizing through the rational analysis of classical authority, the natural properties of music, and contemporary practice.[55] The extraordinary clarity and logicality of the

---

[53] Schmid, 81. Compare *Musica enchiriadis*, ed. Schmid, chap. 3, 7–8.

[54] Law, "The Study of Grammar," 97. See also Irvine, *Making of Textual Culture*, 320–24; Irvine writes that "Alcuin's *De grammatica* differs from its models in an important way: Alcuin's treatise contains an emphasis on definition according to what Alcuin terms the *philosophica disciplina*, that is, according to the rules for definition in dialectic . . ." (321).

[55] I note in passing that Hucbald, in *Musica* 44–46, states that the *customary* musical notation (*consuetudinariae notae*; neumatic notation), in general usage, is not standarized in form and faulty with respect to the precise indication of pitch and interval; it should, therefore, be used only as support to the scientific notation (*artificiales notae*; pitch nota-

entire presentation owes much to specifically Carolingian developments within the grammatical discipline.

Martin Irvine writes that in the early Middle Ages,

> . . . *grammatica* was not simply descriptive, isolating and labeling the parts of its subject matter, but productive of knowledge: it supplied a network of presuppositions, discursive strategies, and rules for argumentation that governed inquiry and provided the grounds of possibility for knowledge. *Grammatica* was thus a paradigm, in Kuhn's sense of a conventional and consensual epistemic model acknowledged in varying degrees of self-consciousness by individual practitioners of a discipline, and a discursive practice that supplied the conditions for knowledge . . . .[56]

Specifically, the grammatical discipline, as practiced in the ninth-century Carolingian empire, provided the procedures for establishing meaning in received texts and for producing new texts. In my opinion, Irvine's description of *grammatica* as a methodological paradigm is illustrated perfectly by developments in the production of music theory texts in the Carolingian ninth century. As I have argued, beginning with Hrabanus Maurus's encyclopedic treatment of *musica disciplina*—prefaced by a traditional statement of the centrality of the grammatical discipline, "the first liberal art"—through the *Scolica enchiriadis*, a full-fledged manual or *ars musica*, Carolingian teachers and writers on the subject of music evaluated and interpreted the texts transmitted through late antiquity, compiling collections of notes and creating independent handbooks that were based heavily on this heritage, but addressed contemporary liturgical practice. To accomplish this they often adapted pragmatic classroom techniques developed for teaching grammar, a discipline which by the late eighth century had become a dynamic force in the production of knowledge. Pythagorean mythology is present in these texts only as a frozen memory, rather than a dynamic basis for the extension of knowledge: number theory is treated as a natural physical property of music, the quantitative basis for the determination of pitch, the quadrivial element of an otherwise grammatical and rhetorical—that is, trivial—activity, the performance of the liturgy.

One final point: These independent texts on music or handbooks, a completely new genre,[57] were produced when they were, during the course of the ninth century, in response to Carolingian efforts to destroy the pre-existing

---

tion), proposed by Hucbald and based directly on the authority of Boethius. See Chartier, 194–97.

[56] Irvine, *The Making of Textual Culture*, 8.

[57] Beginning with Lawrence Gushee's study of genre ("Questions of Genre in Medieval Treatises on Music," in *Gattungen der Musik in Einzeldarstellungen, Gedenkschrift Leo Schrade* [Bern and Munich, 1973], 365–433), musicologists have attempted to characterize these innovative texts, offering uneasy dichotomies based on "theory" versus

sociolinguistic compromise between Latin speakers and uneducated listeners, and to re-regulate spoken and written Latin through the Carolingian territories. The late antique *intellectual* context influenced the structure and content of these texts, but the official Carolingian reaction to the eighth-century Merovingian *sociolinguistic* context made their production a necessity. In chapter 5, I consider, within the general context of ninth-century "literacy" or "textuality," the use of music notation within diagrams accompanying these Carolingian music treatises.

"practice." In my opinion, they represent neither theory nor practice exclusively, but an evolution in pedagogy inspired by developments in the teaching of grammar.

Chapter 5
"Reading" Music: Music as Text in Carolingian Music Treatises

In a section entitled "De litteris communibus," near the beginning of book 1 of *Etymologiae*, Isidore of Seville writes:

> Letters are the indices of things, the signs of words, having such strength that the words of those who are not present speak to us soundlessly. (Indeed, they introduce words through our eyes rather than our ears.) The use of letters was devised for the sake of the memory of things. For in order that things do not fade into oblivion, they are bound in letters, as we are not able to learn all the things there are to learn by listening nor to hold all of this in our memory.[1]

In this passage Isidore mentions two of the attributions of alphabetic writing transmitted through late antiquity: writing as a type of "external" memory, a means of preservation of knowledge; and writing as "soundless" human speech, the "voices of the absent." With regard to the latter, he echoes Augustine, for example, who had written that "words could not be heard by those who were not present; thus reason conceived letters for all of the observed, discrete sounds of the mouth and of language."[2] And in a well-known remark, Cassiodorus praises

---

[1] *Etymologiae*, ed. Lindsay, 1.13: "Litterae autem sunt indices rerum, signa verborum, quibus tanta vis est, ut nobis dicta absentium sine voce loquantur. (Verba enim per oculos non per aures introducunt.) Usus litterarum repertus propter memoriam rerum. Nam ne oblivione fugiant, litteris alligantur. In tanta enim rerum varietate nec disci audiendo poterant omnia, nec memoria contineri." For an extremely cognitive interpretation of this passage, see Gregor Vogt-Spira, "Senses, Imagination, and Literature: Some Epistemological Considerations," in *Rethinking the Medieval Senses: Heritage / Fascination / Frames*, ed. Stephen G. Nichols, Andreas Kablitz, and Alison Calhoun (Baltimore, 2008), 51–72, at 54.

[2] Augustine, *De ordine* 2.12, ed. W. M. Green, Corpus Christianorum Series Latina 29 (Turnhout, 1970), 127: "Sed audiri absentium verba non poterant; ergo illa ratio peperit litteras notatis omnibus oris ac linguae sonis atque discretis."

both writing and the writeable surface (here papyrus) for the ability to "keep the sweet harvest of the mind and restore it to the reader whenever he wants."[3]

The Carolingians, of course, received and nurtured these ideas; a particularly eloquent statement of the importance, and the authority, of the written word is given by Hrabanus Maurus:

No work sees the light which hoary old age
does not destroy or wicked time overturn:
only letters are immortal and ward off death,
only letters in books bring the past to life.
Indeed God's hand carved letters on the rock
that pleased him when he gave his law to the people,
and these letters reveal everything in the world that is,
has been, or may chance to come in the future.[4]

Brian Stock writes that beginning in the Carolingian ninth century, "People began to think of facts not as recorded by texts but as embodied in texts, a change in mentality of major importance . . . The search for facts, hitherto limited to memory, now shifted to the written page."[5] And Rosalind McKitterick and Michel Banniard have carefully documented the use and authority of the written word within the Frankish kingdoms; in particular, McKitterick writes that "there are many more functions and manifestations of literacy, not the least of which is the development of written musical notation . . ."[6]

The development of systems of music notation is unquestionably an aspect of literacy, or what Stock prefers to call "textuality";[7] and "music writing," by process of analogy, was considered by Carolingian teachers and writers to have uses similar to those of alphabetic writing, that is, as "external" memory and as "voiceless" communication. For example, in chapter 6 of *Musica enchiriadis*, daseian pitch notation

---

[3] Cassiodorus, *Varia* 11.38, quoted in Thomas Mathiesen, "Hermes or Clio? The Transmission of Ancient Music Theory," in *Musical Humanism and Its Legacy: Essays in Honor of Claude V. Palisca*, ed. Nancy K. Baker and Barbara Russano Hanning (Stuyvesant, NY, 1992), 3–35, at 5 and n. 3: "ubi apicibus elevatis fecundissima verborum plantata seges fructum mentibus totiens suavissimum reddit."

[4] Peter Godman, *Poetry of the Carolingian Renaissance* (Norman, OK, 1985), 249; Latin original, PL 112.1600–1601.

[5] Stock, *Listening for the Text*, 126. For a critique of some of Stock's positions and a general discussion of the issues involved, see Matthew Innes, "Orality and Literacy in an Early Medieval Society," *Past and Present* 158 (1998): 3–36.

[6] Rosalind McKitterick, *The Carolingians and the Written Word* (Cambridge, 1989), 272–73; Banniard, *Viva Voce*.

[7] Stock, *Listening for the Text*, 144. By textuality, Stock means the uses of texts in specific historical occasions, as opposed to literacy (a generic term of reference) or even "documentation."

is described as allowing beginning students to learn an unknown and, by implication, unheard melody by mean of the signs for the pitches of the gamut.[8] Chapter 7 contains an explicit analogy between alphabetic writing and daseian pitch notation: "practice makes notating or singing pitches as easy as writing and reading letters."[9] And in *Musica* 44, Hucbald of St. Amand introduces his adaptation of Boethius's transmission of Greek pitch notation as follows:

> We now turn to the written musical signs which, placed next to each of the strings, can be quite useful to those who are learning melodies. These signs were devised for the following purpose: just as by means of the letters [of the alphabet] the sounds and basic meaningful parts of the words in a written text can be identified unambiguously by the reader, in the same way it becomes possible to sing at first sight any melody notated with these signs, once they are learned, even without the aid of a teacher.[10]

Hucbald is paraphrasing Boethius (*De institutione musica* 4.3), but the specific reference to the ability of these "signs" to function as an absent teacher, that is, "voiceless singing," is his own contribution.

These examples indicate that the newly developed systems of music notation, or music "writing," were considered by the Carolingians to have many of the traditional properties of alphabetic writing. In this chapter I consider specifically the implications of the appearance of music notation within certain of the diagrams accompanying the texts of *Musica* and *Scolica enchiriadis*. Nancy Phillips describes the *Enchiriadis* diagrams as one of their most significant and yet most overlooked features, providing an unequaled early theoretical source of visual illustration.[11] In an extremely informative chapter she describes and classifies the images and discusses the manuscript tradition;[12] no one, however, has examined carefully the relationship between theoretical text and image produced by their juxtaposition, both in the classroom and on the written page.

---

[8] Schmid, 10: "Dandum quoque aliquid eis est, qui minus adhuc in his exercitati sunt, . . . ignotum melum ex nota eorum qualitate et ordine per signa investigare." Cf. Ziolkowski, *Nota Bene*, 39–41.

[9] *Musica enchiriadis*, trans. Erickson, 6; Schmid, 13: "donec sonos posse notare vel canere non minus quam litteras scribere vel legere ipse usus efficiat."

[10] Chartier, 194: "Nunc ad notas musicas quae unicuique cordarum appositae sunt, non minimum studiosis melodiae conferunt fructum, ordo uertatur. Hae autem ad hanc utilitatem sunt repertae, ut sicut per litteras, uoces et dictiones uerborum recognoscuntur in scripto, ut nullum legentem dubio fallant iudicio, sic per has omne melos adnotatum, etiam sine docente, postquam semel cognitae fuerint, ualeat decantari." For a discussion of the use and meaning of the term *dictio* in the Carolingian ninth century, see Saenger, *Space Between Words*, 89, 113, 121.

[11] See Phillips, "*Musica* and *Scolica Enchiriadis*," 201.

[12] See Phillips, "*Musica* and *Scolica Enchiriadis*," 201–39.

In the most general sense, all of these musical diagrams are graphic commentary, and the use of supplementary visual aids to clarify, illustrate, or explain Carolingian school texts has been studied by Bruce Eastwood, John Contreni, and others. Contreni, for example, writes, "Their essentially pedagogical concern encouraged masters to try to make scientific principles visual in the form of graphs and charts . . . These illustrations are often quite complex. Teachers used them to convey verbal doctrine in images of high visual impact and thus moved between two kinds of cognition . . . while texts may have inspired the images, the images pushed thought beyond the limits imposed by words."[13]

For the most part the non-notated harmonic diagrams found in these handbooks are based on illustrations in *De institutione musica*: Boethius had written that whatever is presented to the sense of sight is more deeply embedded in memory, and his frequent use of visual aids confirms that belief.[14] Diagrams similar to those of *De institutione musica* were undoubtedly used in the classroom by Carolingian teachers and subsequently found their way into the written records of these classes.[15] In content and style these particular visual aids are certainly quadrivial, and thus of the same general type as the visualized "scientific principles" mentioned by Contreni. Paul Ricoeur writes, "Far from yielding less than the original, pictorial activity may be characterized in terms of an 'iconic augmentation,' where the strategy of painting, for example, is to reconstruct reality on the basis of a limited optic alphabet."[16] In my opinion, visual images of this type are iconic, in Ricoeur's sense, strategic transformations of reality that can be more cognitively efficient than text: properly designed, they are directly comprehended. But this cognitive efficiency can entail oversimplification, a transformation of reality in which certain related assumptions, which may or may not be expressed

---

[13] Contreni, "The Pursuit of Knowledge," 125. See also Bruce Eastwood, "Plinian Astronomical Diagrams in the Early Middle Ages," in *Mathematics and Its Application to Science and Natural Philosophy in the Middle Ages*, ed. Edward Grant and John P. Murdoch (Cambridge, 1987), 141–72.

[14] Boethius, *De interpretatione Aristotelis* 2, PL 64.0468: "quatenus quod animo cogitationeque conceptum est oculis expositum memoriae tenacius infigatur." And in *De arithmetica*, discussing his translation of Nicomachus, Boethius notes his use of diagrams for clarification of the text (cf. Bower, *Fundamentals of Music*, xxv and n. 19). On the transmission of *De institutione musica* and the difficulty of correctly rendering Boethian diagrams, see Bower, *Fundamentals of Music*, xxxviii–xliv. See also M. Masi, *Boethian Number Theory: A Translation of the* De institutione arithmetica (Amsterdam, 1983), 14–30, 58–63 (listing manuscripts), 125–27, 131–53, 156–63, 167–72, 177–79, 187–88.

[15] See, for example, *Musica enchiriadis* chap. 11 (Schmid, 29) and chap. 16 (Schmid, 44); and *Scolica enchiriadis* pt. 2 (Schmid, 111) and pt. 3 (Schmid, 131, 137, 145, and 147). See also *Musica Disciplina*, ed. Gushee, chap. 6 (70–77).

[16] Paul Ricoeur, *Interpretation Theory: Discourse and the Surplus of Meaning* (Fort Worth, 1976), 40.

explicitly in the text, are concealed or ignored in order to make a specific point within a pedagogical context.

Consider, for example, figure 1, the Boethian harmonic diagram accompanying the text of chapter 11 of *Musica enchiriadis*, "How from simple symphonies others are composed," and illustrating the concept that the intervals of the perfect fourth (*diatessaron*) and the perfect fifth (*diapente*) "combine" to produce the octave (*diapason*), and that this process is infinitely renewable.[17] The immediate impression is that of simplicity and regularity: the elegant curves joining alphabetically-labeled locations on a vertical linear axis seem to have been constructed with a scientific instrument of measurement like a compass, and suggest geometric certainty. But the impression of simple linearity is misleading: in physical, or acoustical, terms, the process of "combination" of musical intervals requires multiplication of their respective frequency ratios; in this case 4:3 (a perfect fourth) times 3:2 (a perfect fifth) equals 12:6 or 2:1, the frequency ratio of an octave. Expressing frequency ratios as intervals or distances on a vertical line seems to make their compounding self-evident—the fourth and the fifth "add up" to an octave. But this musical interpretation ignores the difficulties in defining scale steps within the Pythagorean system of intonation, which includes two unequal semitones.[18]

Furthermore, the alphabetic locations on the vertical scale, which have been adapted from a Boethian illustration of the divisions of the string of a monochord, do not in this diagram represent specific pitches, but rather "pitch classes," that is, the class of all pitches denoted by the letter A, rather than a specific one of them; this concept is not addressed in the text, however.[19] Another problem with this adaptation is that Boethius worked within an abstract system in which octaves were consistent, whereas the daseian scale of the *Enchiriadis* treatises has an interval pattern designed to be "infinitely renewable" at the interval of a fifth rather than an octave; the resulting presence of "augmented" octaves in the daseian scale is referred to only obliquely in the accompanying text of *Musica*

---

[17] Schmid, 28–29.

[18] The frequency ratio of a Pythagorean whole tone is 9/8; however, the equation for two equal semitones, x-squared = 9/8, does not have a solution in integers: x = 3 divided by 2 times the square root of 2. The two unequal semitones in Pythagorean theory are the diesis or limma (the difference between two whole tones and a perfect fourth, 256/243) and the apotome (slightly larger, the difference between the whole tone and the diesis). The difference between these two semitones is the so-called Pythagorean comma, the difference, for example, between 3/2 to the twelfth power and 2/1, or 6 whole tones and an octave. For a complete discussion of Pythagorean tuning systems, see John Backus, *The Acoustical Foundations of Music*, 2nd ed. (New York and London, 1977), esp. chap. 8, "Intervals, Scales, Tuning, and Temperament," 134–60.

[19] Schmid, 33: "Unde et in Virgilio apud Elisium Orpheus obloquitur numeris septem discrimina vocum." Note that the letters descend from "A."

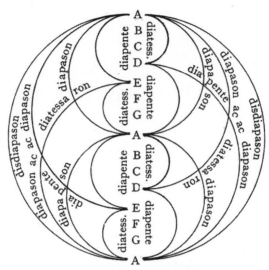

FIGURE 1. An adaptation of a Boethian harmonic diagram illustrating the "combination" of the intervals of the fourth and the fifth to produce the octave. The alphabetic locations on the vertical scale represent "pitch classes." Reproduced from Schmid, 29, with the permission of the Bayerische Akademie der Wissenschaften, Musikhistorische Kommission.

enchiriadis.[20] Undeniably the visual and cognitive impact is that of quadrivial certainty, but the relationship between the visual iconicity of figure 1 and its textual frame is complicated and potentially misleading.

I begin consideration of the "notated" examples in these handbooks with the illustrated presentation of the eighteen pitches of the gamut and their written signs — the so-called "daseian" note forms — found in the early version of the first *Enchiriadis* handbook (fig. 2).[21] This diagram owes its inspiration not only to *musica disciplina* as transmitted by Boethius and others, but also to *ars grammatica*. Priscian, for example, after making a careful distinction between the element of speech, the indivisible sound, and its written image, the letter, enumerates the defining characteristics of an individual letter: its name (*nomen*), its written sign (*figura*), and its sound or pronunciation (*potestas, pronuntiatio*).[22] These same characteristics (attributed by Alcuin to Donatus) are presented in Alcuin's

---

[20] Schmid, 31: "Sane non ab uno tantum quolibet sono ad quartum vel quintum aut octavum consonantia fit . . ." On the the daseian scale, see *Musica enchiriadis and Scolica enchiriadis*, trans. Erickson xxx–xxxii; Phillips, "*Musica* and *Scolica Enchiriadis*," chap. 11; and n. 32 below. The augmented octaves of the daseian scale are increased by a limma plus a comma, or an apotome.

[21] Schmid, 5.

[22] Priscian, *Institutio grammatica*, ed. Keil, Grammatici Latini 2–3, 2.6–9.

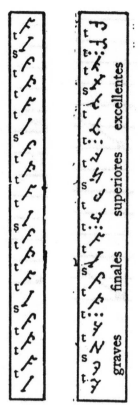

FIGURE 2. Left: the four note-forms of the daseian scale arranged in tetrachords having the same internal intervallic relationship of (T-S-T). Right: the daseian scale with inversions and rotations indicating different pitches within a pitch class; the four basic tetrachords (*graves, finales, superiores*, and *excellentes*) are indicated. Reproduced from Schmid, 5, with the permission of the Bayerische Akademie der Wissenschaften, Musikhistorische Kommission.

Grammatica, written in the form of a conversation between two students, a Saxon and a Frank, and a teacher.[23] There follows a detailed discussion of each letter, its written sign, and its use in various particular cases. This is exactly the methodology of the *Enchiriadis* treatises; and here as well, the distinction between the sounded note and its written name is for the most part carefully observed.[24] It is reasonable to assume that the dialogue recorded in Alcuin's *Grammatica* originated in the classroom; as Contreni writes, the dialectical question-and-response

---

[23] Alcuin, *Grammatica*, PL 101.855: "Fr. Ut reor, in Donato legimus, tria accidisse litteris: nomen, figuram, potestatem."

[24] See Sullivan, "*Nota* and *Notula*," 88–94.

format was extremely useful in a classroom situation in which students learned by repetition and memorization.[25] The pronunciation exercises recorded in such grammar handbooks were originally conducted orally, and doubtless the same is true of the expositions in the *Enchiriadis* treatises of the notes of the gamut, their organization into tetrachords, and other elementary material. In *Musica enchiriadis*, for example, we find the following introduction to an illustration: "In order to confirm what has been said, both audibly and visibly, we need to make another little diagram using the same notes."[26]

According to Pierre Riché, beginning in the last years of the eighth century, instruction in Carolingian classrooms was aided by instruments such as the psaltery and the organ,[27] and specific references to the use of musical instruments to illustrate tonal relationships occur in both *Enchiriadis* treatises.[28] References to singing also appear throughout these treatises; a typical example is the following exchange: "Student: May I hear you sing these notes? Teacher: Listen as I sing."[29] Explicit references to audible demonstrations, whether by instrument or by voice, certainly distinguish the notated examples from the traditional harmonic diagrams adapted from Boethius or other late antique sources. Referring to Boethius's use of diagrams, Phillips writes, "The teaching of vocal skills or the illustration of acoustical phenomena with examples chosen from the music of his own era would have been unthinkable to Boethius . . . The study of music in Boethius is directed to the comprehension by the intellect of the mathematical bases of musical phenomena . . ."[30]

Even in this elementary notated example, however, there exists a complicated relationship between text and image. The column on the left of figure 2 repeats the same set of four written symbols as representations of pitch classes, while the column on the right uses rotated and inverted versions of these symbols as a visual indication that they represent different pitches within a specific pitch class, a procedure derived from Greek instrumental notation. By way of explanation, the accompanying text simply refers to the "natural" succession of repeated groups of four notes or tetrachords—having the same internal intervallic relationship of (T-S-T)—in which the written symbols for pitches occupying the same position

---

[25] Contreni, "The Pursuit of Knowledge," 124.

[26] Schmid, 14: "Ergo ut, quod dicitur, et audiendo et videndo comprobetur, alia rursus descriptiuncula per neumam eandem fiat."

[27] Riché, *Écoles et Enseignement*, 241.

[28] See, for example, Schmid, 26–27 and Schmid, 61.

[29] Schmid, 62: "D: . . . eos sonos te canente audiam. M: Ecce canam." On the interpretation of the verb *canere* in these treatises, see Phillips, "*Musica* and *Scolica Enchiriadis*," 235–36. Phillips agrees that the directions to sing or listen were originally intended to be taken literally.

[30] Phillips, "*Musica* and *Scolica Enchiriadis*," 201–2.

in the tetrachord are "almost the same."[31] As I mentioned previously, the resulting scale is fifth-based, not octave-based, and contains augmented octaves.[32]

I turn now to what I believe to be the entirely new status of some of these musical diagrams or examples, as we would commonly call them.[33] As I have argued, the less complicated "notated" examples that serve to introduce the notes of the daseian gamut and elementary relationships between them are very like the pronunciation exercises found near the beginnings of grammar handbooks. The more complicated notated diagrams, however, go well beyond the simple grammatical paradigm, and it will be instructive to examine several of them in detail. In particular, I am interested in examining the dialectic—a process of reinterpretation—that exists between text and image when pitch notation is an essential part of the representation: such examples contain within themselves information that is both iconic *and* semantic, an interplay of visibility and legibility. They are intended to be read, not metaphorically but literally—either in a classroom situation or silently alone.[34]

I begin with the musical example in chapter 11 of *Musica enchiriadis* (fig. 3), and its companion in *Scolica enchiriadis* (fig. 4).[35] The principle to be illustrated is the same as in figure 1, the formation of compound symphonies, in particular,

---

[31] Schmid, 6: "Igitur quia, ut dictum est, eiusdem conditionis quattuor et quattuor natura statuit, ita et notae pene sunt eadem."

[32] In modern notation, the eighteen pitches of the daseian gamut (arranged in designated tetrachords, from lowest to highest) are *graves*: GG, A, B♭, C; *finales*: D, E, F, G; *superiores*: a, b, c, d; *excellentes*: e, f#, g, a¹; plus b¹ and c#¹. Augmented octaves occur at B♭ to b, F to f#, and c to c#¹. The octave-based modal system did not come into general usage until the eleventh century; it is reasonable to assume, as does Nancy Phillips, that the pitches in the daseian gamut represented contemporary practice, based on Pythagorean intonation. See Phillips, *"Musica* and *Scolica Enchiriadis,"* chap. 11, "The Dasia Notation and the Chant Repertoire."

[33] For a fascinating discussion of music exemplarity and what it means to "read" a musical example, see Cristle Collins Judd, *Reading Renaissance Music Theory: Hearing with the Eyes* (Cambridge, 2000), esp. "Hearing with the Eyes: The Nature of Musical Exemplarity," 5–16. Judd studies, within the context of sixteenth-century print culture, the complicated web of external references surrounding the use of specific repertory within the texts of several music theory treatises. See also Sam Barrett, "Music and Writing: On the Compilation of Paris Bibliothèque Nationale lat. 1154," *Early Music History* 16 (1997): 55–96.

[34] Phillips writes, "To perceive the *Enchiriadis* treatises as being read as we would read a treatise today, that is, silently and by an individual, is almost certainly incorrect" (*"Musica* and *Scolica Enchiriadis,"* 236). But nonetheless, through the process of instruction, that is exactly what eventually happens. Judd, *Reading Renaissance Music Theory*, 8, writes of notated examples that at times "the notation is meant to be 'read' and 'heard,' . . ."

[35] Schmid, 32, 91, respectively.

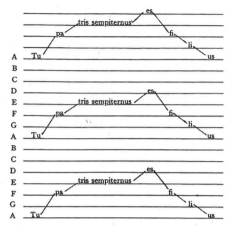

Figure 3. Parallel melodic motion at the interval of an octave. In the column at the left of the diagram, pitch classes are indicated rather than precise pitch notation, as the daseian scale does not have consistent reduplication at the octave. Reproduced from Schmid, 32, with the permission of the Bayerische Akademie der Wissenschaften, Musikhistorische Kommission.

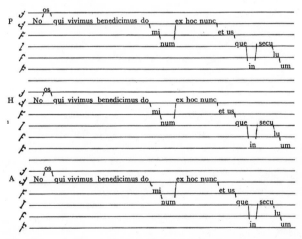

Figure 4. Parallel melodic motion at the interval of an octave. The letters P, H, and A indicate different registers, but the melodic phrases are "falsely" notated: the full daseian scale, with its inversions and rotations. is not used. Reproduced from Schmid, 91, with the permission of the Bayerische Akademie der Wissenschaften, Musikhistorische Kommission.

the octave. Now, however, the harmonic theory has been translated into liturgical practice: in figure 3, the same vertical linear array, with its alphabetic units, is presented, but here each alphabetic unit is placed next to a horizontal line representing that pitch class. The melodic contour is formed by the syllables of the fifteenth verse of the Matins hymn *Te deum*, placed at points on the horizontal array and connected successively by straight lines. The diagram—which is introduced by a statement of the "oneness of sound" heard among voices at a distance of an octave above and below a principal voice[36]—is a visual demonstration of parallel melodic motion at the octave. Specific pitch is not indicated, undoubtedly because the daseian scale of the treatise does not have consistent reduplication at the interval of an octave. This is a case in which precise pitch notation would contradict the principle being demonstrated visually. In figure 4, a setting of the Vespers antiphon verse "Sed nos qui vivimus" (Psalm 113:26), daseian notation replaces the alphabetic letters, but the example is "falsely" notated: the full daseian scale, with its inversions and rotations, is not used. Instead the original four daseian symbols are duplicated at the octave, with the letters P, H, and A indicating different registers. Yet in both cases the visual impact of the vertical representation of parallel vocal motion is undeniable: vocal unity at the octave (ignoring timbral differences) is heard relatively easily, but parallel vocal motion projected onto a vertical axis is a striking visual model for aural cognition. It is first seen, and then heard.[37] In addition, for each of the three vocal lines, the projection onto a vertical axis makes explicit the pitch relationships implicit in the daseian notation.

Figure 5, from chapter 12 of *Musica enchiriadis*, incorporates the visual model for parallel vocal motion established in the previous chapter, but in this case the melodic motion is not strictly parallel.[38] The principle involved is successive modal transposition by a whole tone or a semitone through the interval of a fifth. The same melodic phrase from the *Te deum* is presented, with straight lines (apparently originally in five different colors)[39] connecting successive syllables. But here the vertical placeholders of the previous diagram have been replaced with symbols indicating specific pitches of the daseian scale. The text preceding the

---

[36] Schmid, 31: "Porro maxima simphonia diapason dicitur, quod in ea perfectior ceteris consonantia fiat, ut sive ab acutiore sive a graviore incipias, vox, quam octavo ordine in celsiorem vel humiliorem mutaveris, ad primam vocem unisona habeatur, ita canendo."

[37] I refer again to Intons-Peterson's experimental results on auditory imagery and cognition, cited at the end of chapter 1, to the effect that what a subject has learned to expect affects what is "heard"; see Intons-Peterson, "Components of Auditory Imagery," 63.

[38] Schmid, 36.

[39] Schmid, 36: "Sternatur ut prius veluti disposita cordarum series et idem melos, quod nunc in diapente simphonia designatum est, quaternis vel quinis colorum descriptionibus exprimatur . . ."

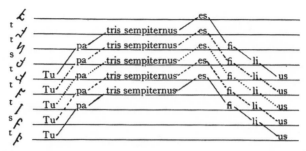

FIGURE 5. Transposition of a melodic phrase by a tone or semitone. The melodic lines appear to be strictly parallel; the melodic differences must be read from the daseian notation. Reproduced from Schmid, 36, with the permission of the Bayerische Akademie der Wissenschaften, Musikhistorische Kommission.

diagram explains the underlying principle, that the form of the melody changes as it is shifted upward by a whole tone or a semitone, a fact that is said to be made "visible" in the diagram.[40] But that is exactly what is not *seen* unless the notation is actually read, for without the notation the image seems to be a representation of exact parallel motion. Here the visual model records and adds notation—scalar identification—to an exercise in singing and in aural perception of the placement of tones and semitones particular to each of the four melodic transpositions. The written signs, like alphabetic letters, become the means by which the principle of modal transposition is read and understood.

Figure 6, a diagram from chapter 13 of *Musica enchiriadis*,[41] illustrates a type of polyphony known as organum, in this case two simultaneous vocal lines at the interval of a perfect fourth. The same *Te deum* verse is used, and daseian pitches are indicated on the vertical axis. The visually obvious fact that parallel motion between the two voices is abandoned on the last two syllables of the phrase is not mentioned in the surrounding text, but the fact that this melodic adjustment in the organal or lower voice avoids a tritone (the so-called "devil in music") between the tritus of the graves tetrachord (b-flat) and the deuterus of the tetrachord of finals (e-natural) can be *read* from the daseian notation. In a related example in chapter 17, an organal setting at the fourth of the sequence "Rex caeli," the preceding text describes in detail a "certain law" for this procedure that avoids potential tritones. The diagram is introduced as as follows: "In order to clarify these things, they are placed in a diagram, to the extent that it can

---

[40] Schmid, 36: ". . . *videbisque* eandem melodiae formam in transpositione sua manere non posse, sed per epogdoi vel semitonii distantiam modum unumquemque in alium transmutari ita" (my italics).

[41] Schmid, 38

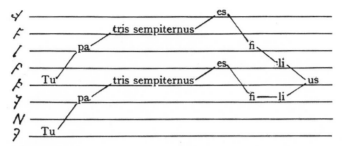

FIGURE 6. A notated example of organum at the interval of a fourth. The lack of parallel motion is ignored in the text, but the need for the alteration in order to avoid a tritone can be read from the daseian notation. Reproduced from Schmid, 38, with the permission of the Bayerische Akademie der Wissenschaften, Musikhistorische Kommission.

be made visible."[42] But it is the solution that is presented; just as in figure 6, the potential problem must be carefully *read* from the daseian notation. It is interesting to note that the assertion that there are facts about music that can be heard but not seen seems to contradict what Regino of Prüm, writing at the end of the ninth century, states on the subject of the liberal arts:

> There are, indeed, seven liberal arts, of which three are grouped together by reason and natural meaning—that is, grammar, rhetoric, and dialectic. They are not seen by the eye, neither are they shown by the finger because the meaning of these arts lies in discourse, while discourse—that is, human speech—can be heard and cannot be seen. The remaining four—that is, arithmetic, geometry, music, and astronomy—are never clearly perceived by the mind unless they are seen by the eye . . .[43]

In quoting a traditional distinction between the trivial and the quadrivial liberal arts, Regino has failed to take into account a development that seems to have been quite clear to the Carolingian teacher, and which I examined in detail in chapter 4: during the course of the ninth century, harmonic theory, that is, the

---

[42] Schmid, 49: "Quae ut lucidiora fiant, exempli descriptione statuantur, prout possit fieri sub aspectum."

[43] Regino of Prüm, *De harmonica institutione*, ed. Edna Marie Le Roux, "The *De harmonica* and *Tonarius* of Regino of Prüm" (Ph.D. diss., Catholic University of America, 1985), 58: "Septem quippe sunt liberales disciplinae, quarum tres, id est, grammatica, rhetorica et dialectica, ratione et naturali sensu colliguntur, non oculo videntur, aut digito monstrantur, quia earum vis in sermone est, sermo autem, id est, humana locutio, audiri potest, videri non potest. Reliquae quatuor, id est, arithmetica, geometrica, musica, et astrologia nequequam animo ad liquidum percipiuntur, nisi oculo videantur et digito demonstrentur."

quantitative basis for the determination of pitch, becomes the quadrivial element of an otherwise grammatical and rhetorical—that is, trivial—activity, the performance of the liturgy. The Boethian harmonic diagrams fit well into Regino's dichotomy; these musical diagrams incorporating music notation do not.

Chapter 14 contains an elaboration of figure 6 with octaval doubling below the principal voice and above the organal voice (fig. 7).[44] There is, however, no daseian pitch notation, undoubtedly because of the difficulties involved in octaval doubling using the pitches of the daseian scale, so the potential problem of a tritone can no longer be "read."[45] In this case, notation would present a problem that the improvisatory practice, in the classroom or elsewhere, of octaval doubling above and below specified pitches would not encounter.[46] In the actual practice of organum, only the chant melody would be notated. These musical diagrams of organum, however, were produced in a pedagogical context; in both cases the graphic commentary accesses information not readily available from the text alone: figure 6 textualizes the problem of the tritone occurring in parallel organum at the interval of a fourth; and figure 7, although disguising the scalar problem of an augmented octave, projects onto a vertical plane the relative motion between the four separate voices, an image of high visual and cognitive impact.

In summary, figures 3, 4, and 7 are iconic, in Ricoeur's sense: the process of transferring the temporal properties of vocal performance to the spatial properties of a diagram brings to the foreground a visually striking abstraction of parallel motion at the interval of an octave. Like the harmonic diagram (fig. 1), to paraphrase Contreni, they have visual impact beyond the limits imposed by hearing.

On the other hand, when daseian pitch notation is an essential part of the representation, as in figures 5 and 6, the examples are not merely visually iconic. They, like the text surrounding them, are meant to be "read"—either in a classroom situation or silently alone—and discussed. Research in auditory imagery has shown that through a process of "subvocalization" we can hear sounds in our heads that we cannot actually produce.[47] In other words, these examples, once embedded in a text, preserve the analogy between alphabetic writing and music notation. As I have shown, however, the relationship between textual frame and image is complicated, even in the most iconic examples. And this dialectic, which arises naturally as part of a classroom performance, becomes all the more

---

[44] Schmid, 39.

[45] A related diagram in part 2 of *Scolica enchiriadis* (Schmid, 100) is "falsely" notated, that is, the same daseian symbols are used in different registers.

[46] The same principle is illustrated in *Scolia enchiriadis* using the Vespers antiphon "Sed nos qui vivimus" (Schmid, 100). Again a subset of daseian symbols is duplicated at the octave to disguise the problem of augmented octaves in the full daseian scale.

[47] See, for example, Alan D. Baddeley, *Essentials of Human Memory* (Hove, 1999), 53–54.

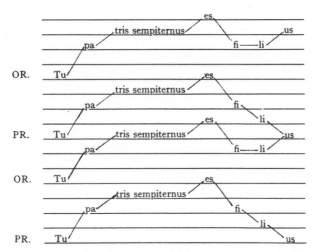

FIGURE 7. Organum at the fourth with octaval doubling above and below the principal voice. The example is not notated, undoubtedly because the daseian scale does not have consistent reduplication at the interval of an octave. Reproduced from Schmid, 39, with the permission of the Bayerische Akademie der Wissenschaften, Musikhistorische Kommission.

obvious when both *word*—spoken or sung—and *diagram* are "textualized," a process that separates the actual event from its interpretation: the technological advances of Carolingian literacy allow the "soundless" voices of teachers and singers to be read and discussed, even twelve centuries after the fact.

Conclusion

It seems certain that an appreciation of similarity is universal in human cognition. In particular, research on analogy and metaphor has shown that the process of mapping structure from one domain to another is basic to human understanding. As Gentner and Jeziorski write, "This structure mapping, a theory of human processing of analogy and similarity, is a type of mapping of knowledge of one field (the base) into another (the target) such that a system of relations that holds among the base objects also holds among the target objects . . . The corresponding objects in the base and target need not resemble each other; rather, object correspondences are determined by like roles in the matching relational structures."[1] Furthermore, as Holyoak, Gentner, and Kokinov write, discussing the process of analogy, "If we consider what it means to be human, certain cognitive capabilities loom large, capabilities that subserve language, art, music, invention, and science. Precisely when these capabilities arose in the course of human evolution is unclear, but it seems likely they were well developed at least fifty thousand years ago . . ."[2] That is, the relevance of modern research on human cognitive processes to a historical study located in Greek and Roman antiquity, late antiquity, and the early Middle Ages is clear.

In the preceding chapters, I have studied a particular type of postulated similarity: the analogy between the relational structure of human speech—the base—and the relational structure of musical sound—the target. This association, as I have indicated, goes back in time at least to Hippias the Sophist in the fifth century B.C.E. I have argued, extending the work of David Olson, that this analogical process began with Greek alphabetic writing and was subsequently extended to Latin: the analytical properties of alphabetic writing—discreteness, finiteness, and combinatorial power—that were first applied to the conceptualization of speech were subsequently applied, by process of analogy, to the conceptualization of musical sound. I have discussed in chapters one through three the following postulated structures and structural mappings:

---

[1] Gentner and Jeziorski, "The Shift from Metaphor to Analogy in Western Science," 448–49.

[2] Keith J. Holyoak, Dedre Gentner, and Boicho N. Kokinov, "Introduction: The Place of Analogy in Cognition," in *The Analogical Mind: Perspectives from Cognitive Science*, ed. eidem (Cambridge, MA, 2001), 1–19, at 1.

Speech (The Base):

Elements of speech: discrete units of sound corresponding to alphabetic letters

Physical material of speech: articulate (writeable) sound

Combinatorial principles of speech: the rules of the grammatical discipline

Music (The Target):

Elements of music: phthongi, discrete measured (that is, pitched) notes

Physical material of music: attuned or melodic sound

Combinatorial principles of music: the rules of the harmonic discipline

The proper movement of combinations of the elements of speech is described as *recte loquendi*, while the proper movement of the elements of music is described as *bene modulandi*.

Following detailed analyses of the fundamental structural similarities, I argued in chapter 4 that by the Carolingian ninth century the grammatical discipline, which had provided a structural model for the study of musical sound, had become a methodological paradigm for the study of liturgical music, leading among other things to the development of musical handbooks or treatises similar in style and procedure to grammatical handbooks or treatises. Finally, in my fifth chapter I presented evidence indicating the similarity in function of musical notation to alphabetic writing in the textualization of classroom performance: written musical examples were in fact intended to be read as text when embedded within theoretical discussions of musical sound.

Michel Banniard has written eloquently about the general context in which the specific developments described in chapters four and five occurred, stressing the absolute priority of grammar in this process.[3] He identifies three levels of transmission within this secular evolution: a fossilized level corresponding to antique mythology; a static level corresponding to the oratorical rules of antique eloquence; and a dynamic level corresponding to the science of the grammarian, the methodological paradigm for the extension of knowledge.[4] Banniard's fossilized

---

[3] Banniard, *Genèse culturelle*, 216.

[4] Banniard, *Genèse culturelle*, 218: "Le chemin parcouru entre le Vᵉ et le VIIIᵉ siècle . . . conduit à un monde culturel nouveau, celui du Moyen Âge . . . Trois niveaux caractérisent cette évolution séculaire: un niveau fossile . . .; un niveau rémanent . . .; un niveau dynamique . . . Ainsi, la mythologie antique n'est préservée qu'accessoirement et ne perdure que dans les marges de la culture, savoir vain et figé. En revanche, les règles

level is represented in my discussion by the Pythagorean foundational mythology for the musical discipline, present only as a frozen memory in ninth-century Carolingian treatises. At the static level, the rules for proper discourse and argumentation were certainly applied in learned ninth-century discussions of music. And at the dynamic level, the science of the grammarian provided a methodological paradigm for Carolingian adaptation and extension of transmitted knowledge of the musical discipline to contemporary liturgical requirements.

In my introduction I mentioned the selective nature of the analogical process in which certain properties or characteristics are highlighted and others — possibly very significant ones — are ignored. I conclude by mentioning very briefly an important dissimilarity that is not directly addressed in the traditional postulation of structural similarities between speech as base and music as target: musical signification or meaning. As Jenefer Robinson writes, "Our paradigms for systems of meaning are languages, but without specially introduced conventions . . . musical phrases and chords do not normally have conventional meanings as words and sentences in a language do."[5] Kofi Agawu elaborates as follows:

> For language to provide a useful model for musical analysis, it must do at least three things: first, it must explain the laws that govern the moment-by-moment succession of events in a piece, that is, the syntax of music. Second and consequently, it must explain the constraints affecting organization at higher levels — the levels of sentence, paragraph, chapter, and beyond. . . . Third, it must demonstrate, rather than merely assume, that music represents a bona fide system of communication . . .[6]

It is certainly correct, as Robinson states, that the meaning of a musical phrase cannot be determined in exactly the same way as the meaning of a sentence; music must have its own set of conventions to represent "a bona fide system of communication," as Agawu requires. Hucbald implicitly recognizes this fact, writing:

> Just as all the words in a language can be expressed through their elements, the letters, and nothing can be said without the use of the elements, thanks to their diligence the ancients have provided all melodies with certain basic

---

oratoires de l'ancienne eloquence, même déchues de leur primauté passée, sont l'objet d'une transmission active. Enfin, la science du grammairien, mise au service de nouveaux langages, fait surgir des limbes de l'analphabétisme des ethnies jusque-là confinées dans la plus pure oralité."

[5] Introduction, in *Music and Meaning*, ed. Jenefer Robinson (Ithaca and London, 1997), 4. See both this collection of articles and Kofi Agawu, *Playing with Signs: A Semiotic Interpretation of Classic Music* (Princeton, 1991), for lively and thought-provoking discussions of the topic of musical meaning and analysis.

[6] Agawu, *Playing with Signs*, 9.

formulas, subject to precise rules, that permit the errorless execution of everything that is sung and exclude anything that does not make sense.[7]

But here, Hucbald's emphasis is on musical syntax, as described by Agawu, and the proper arrangement of the elements of music into successively higher levels, not the communicative powers of music per se.

Indeed, the question of musical meaning or signification is addressed only indirectly in the ninth-century treatises I have considered, and can be examined under the following subheadings: 1. the meaning or signification of (untexted) music; 2. the "ethos" or emotive power of (untexted) music; and 3. the appropriate relationship of music to text in a musical setting of that text.

1. In the Pythagorean-Platonic tradition, the "meaning" of music is quite simply cosmic: the numerical ordering of the universe according to the fundamental ratios 2:1, 3:2, and 4:3, corresponding in music to the perfect consonances. Musical "syntax," to use Agawu's term, is given by the laws of celestial harmony. Boethius, of course, transmits this tradition, writing in *De institutione musica* 1.1: "What Plato said can be recognized to be correct: the soul of the universe was joined together according to musical harmony."[8] Aurelian echoes this thought in the final chapter of *Musica disciplina*: "The very world and the sky above us, according to the doctrine of philosophers, are said to carry within themselves the sound of musical harmony."[9] An even more eloquent formulation is found in the penultimate chapter of *Musica enchiriadis*: "Through these numerical relationships, by which unlike sounds concord with each other, the eternal harmony of life and of the cohesiveness of the elements and of the whole world will unite with material entities."[10] *Scolica enchiriadis*, on the other hand, emphasizes the strictly mathematical signification of music in the following exchange between teacher and student — *magister* (M) and *discipulus* (D):

> D: How is harmony born of mother arithmetic, and is harmony the same thing as music?

---

[7] Chartier, 152: "Unde et elementa uel ptongos eosdem nuncuparunt, quod scilicet, quemadmodum litterarum elementis sermonum cuncta multiplicitas coartatur, et quicquid dici potest, per eas digeritur, ita sollerti procurauerunt industria, ut inmensitas cantilenarum quaedam haberet exordia, et ipsa certo moderamine comprehensa, per quae quicquid canendum foret, sine ullo errore procederet, nihilque in eis esset quod non omni prorsus rationabilitate uigeret."

[8] *De institutione musica*, ed. Friedlein, 180: "Hinc etiam internosci potest, quod non frustra a Platone dictum sit, mundi animam musica convenientia fuisse coniunctam."

[9] *Musica Disciplina*, ed. Gushee, 132: "Etenim et ipse mundus et caelum supra nos iuxta philosophorum dogma gestare insemet dicuntur armonie sonoritatem."

[10] Schmid, 56: ". . . quodque isdem numerorum partibus, quibus sibi collati inaequales soni concordant, et vitae cum corporibus et compaginantiae elementorum totiusque mundi concordia aeterna coierit."

> M: Harmony is deemed the concordant mixture of different musical tones; music is the theory of that concord. Just like the other mathematical disciplines, it [music] is connected in all respects to this theory of numbers, so it is proper that they [these disciplines] be understood through numbers.[11]

Hucbald of St. Amand agrees, writing: "[The student] will then discover how all the elements of the musical discipline—or everything that deals with the knowledge of consonant intervals—are ordered according to the most harmonious science of numbers and how all created things are assembled and unified in conformity with numerical law."[12]

2. Boethius also transmits in *De institutione musica* 1.1 a second element of the Pythagorean-Platonic tradition, the "ethos" or affective and emotive powers of music: "Plato holds music of optimal character, modestly formed, to be an important guardian of the republic; thus it should be temperate, simple, and manly, rather than effeminate, violent, or inconstant."[13] This ability of music to affect human behavior is seconded and extended by Aurelian: "Music moves the passions of men and stimulates the emotions into a different state. In war it restores the aggressiveness of the combatants; and the more vehement the din of the trumpet, the braver is the spirit made for battle. The sound of music also influences beasts, serpents, birds, and dolphins . . ."[14] And *Music enchiriadis* briefly describes the responses of birds and beasts to music: "Wild animals and birds are said to be attracted by some modes more than others, but it is not simple to investigate the whys and wherefores of such things."[15]

3. Finally, what is the appropriate relationship between a text and a musical setting of that text? This question lies beyond the scope of Boethius's treatise, for example, but is presumably of considerable interest in a discussion of ninth-century liturgical song. As Calvin Bower has pointed out, both *Musica* and *Scolica enchiriadis* use Latin grammatical terms—*particula, comma, colon*—to discuss

---

[11] Schmid, 106–7: "D: Quomodo ex arithmetica matre gignitur armonia, et an eadem est armonia quae musica? M: Armonia putatur concordabilis inaequalium vocum commixtio, musica ipsius concordationis ratio. Quae sicut per omnia numerorum rationi coniuncta est, atque ceterae mathesis disciplinae, ita per numeros oportet ut intellegantur."

[12] Chartier, 136.

[13] *De institutione musica*, ed. Friedlein, 181: "Idcirco magnam esse custodiam rei publicae Plato arbitratur musicam optime moratam pudenterque coniunctam, ita ut sit modesta ac simplex et mascula nec effeminata nec fera nec varia."

[14] *Musica Disciplina*, ed. Gushee, 132: "Musica enim hominum movet affectus, in diversum habitum provocat sensum. In bello quoque pugnantium vires reficit et quanto vehementior fuerit tube clangor, tanto animus ad certamen efficitur fortior. Bestias quoque serpentes volucros ac delfines suum ad auditum provocat."

[15] Schmid, 59: "Dicuntur ferae atque aves modis quibusdam delectari magis quam aliis, sed quare et quomodo haec aliave sint, non facile investigatur."

successive organizational levels of liturgical chant.[16] And as one would expect, these divisions and levels are determined by corresponding divisions and levels within the text. *Scolica enchiriadis* goes further, describing what is referred to as "numerose canere," a means of articulating grammatical phrases by lengthening the musical duration of certain syllables.[17] Beyond mere formal considerations, the question of the appropriate character of a musical setting of a text is addressed in the final chapter of *Musica enchiriadis*: "The emotions of the subjects that are sung about should correspond to the effect of the melody, so that tranquil melodies correspond to tranquil subjects, cheerful melodies to delightful subjects, and appropriate melodies to sad things; and let harsh things that are said or done be expressed by harsh melodies. Let melodies be sudden, clamorous, rapid, and otherwise formed according to various other qualities of emotions and events."[18] That is, the melodic component of a song takes its meaning and significance from the text of that song. The emotional power of music is recognized, but in a particular melodic setting of a text, the character of the melody must suit the character of the text.

To summarize, to these Carolingian writers the purely melodic component of liturgical song is and should be subservient to its text, "the musical art for the embellishment of ecclesiastical song."[19] But for the Carolingians, the meaning and signification of untexted "absolute" music is theological, the divinely created unchanging numerical order of the universe, as eloquently described in *Scolica enchiriadis*: "Numerical relationships produce all that is admirable in a delightful rhythm or in proper melody or in any rhythmical motion. The sound of music is ephemeral; numerical structure, however, which is altered through the physicality of musical tones and the condition of motion, endures."[20]

My narrative began in chapter 1 with Greek alphabetic writing developed ca. 750 B.C.E., and ended in chapter 5 with another type of writing: a system of musical notation developed during the Carolingian ninth century. I hope that my interest in the process of transcription of speech and music and the ways in which the theorization of the Greek and Latin languages influenced learned discussions of musical sound will be shared by readers of this essay. Daniel Leech-Wilkinson

---

[16] Bower, "The Grammatical Model of Musical Understanding in the Middle Ages," 134–39. Cf. Ziolkowski, *Nota Bene*, 188–205.

[17] Cf. Schmid, 86–89.

[18] Schmid, 58: "Nam affectus rerum, quae canuntur oportet, ut imitetur cantionis effectus; ut in tranquillis rebus tranquillae sint neumae, laetisonae in iucundis, merentes in tristibus; quae dura sint dicta vel facta, duris neumis exprimi; subitis, clamosis, incitatis et ad ceteras qualitates affectuum et eventuum deformatis; . . ."

[19] Schmid, 56: "quaedam artis musicae pro ornatu ecclesiasticorum carminum."

[20] Schmid, 113–14: ". . . quicquid rithmi delectabile prestant sive in modulationibus seu in quibuslibet rithmicis motibus, totum numerus efficit. Et voces quidem celeriter transeunt, numeri autem, qui corporea vocum et motuum materia decolorantur, manent."

has written eloquently that "musicologists should feel free . . . to study medieval music, or any other music, any way they find rewarding. The responsibility is theirs to pass on that sense of fascination and excitement to readers, performers, listeners."[21] I trust that I have met this responsibility in writing about a subject I find to be absolutely fascinating and endlessly exciting, the theorization of musical sound. "Huiusce oratiunculae ponamus hic finem."[22]

---

[21] Daniel Leech-Wilkinson, *The Modern Invention of Medieval Music: Scholarship, Ideology, Performance* (Cambridge, 2002), 260.

[22] Schmid, 59.

Works Cited

Primary Sources

Alcuin. *Grammatica*. PL 101.849–902.

Anonyma de Musica Scripta Bellermanniana. Ed. Dietmar Najock. Leipzig, 1975.

Aristides Quintilianus De Musica. Ed. R. P. Winnington-Ingram. Leipzig, 1963.

Aristotle. *Metaphysics Books I–IX*. Ed. G. P. Goold and trans. Hugh Tredennick. Loeb Classical Library. Cambridge, MA, and London, 1933; repr. 1996.

———. *On Interpretation*. Ed. and trans. Hugh Tredennick. Loeb Classical Library. Cambridge, MA, and London, 1938; repr. 1996.

———. *On the Soul*. Ed. J. P. Goold. Loeb Classical Library. Cambridge, MA, and London, 1936; repr. 1995.

———. *Poetics*. Ed. and trans. Stephen Halliwell. Loeb Classical Library. Cambridge, MA, and London, 1995; repr. 1999.

Aristoxenus. *The Harmonics of Aristoxenus*. Ed. Henry Stewart Macran. Oxford, 1902; repr. Hildesheim, Zurich, and New York, 1990.

Augustine. *De ordine*. Ed. W. M. Green. Corpus Christianorum Series Latina 29. Turnhout, 1970.

Aurelian of Réôme. *Aurelianus Reomensis: Musica Disciplina*. Ed. Lawrence Gushee. Corpus Scriptorum de Musica 21. Rome, 1975.

Boethius, Anicius Manlius Severinus. *Anicii Manlii Torquati Severini Boetii De institutione arithmetica libri duo, De institutione musica libri quinque*. Ed. G. Friedlein. Leipzig, 1867.

———. *Commentarii in Aristoteli Peri Hermeneias*. Ed. C. Meiser. 2 vols. Leipzig, 1877–1880.

———. *Fundamentals of Music*. Intro., notes, and trans. Calvin M. Bower. New Haven, 1989.

Calcidius. *Timaeus a Calcidio Translatus Commentarioque Instructus*. Ed. J. H. Waszink. London and Leiden, 1975.

Capella, Martianus. *De nuptiis Philologiae et Mercurii*. Ed. Adolf Dick. Stuttgart, 1969.

———. *De nuptiis Philologiae et Mercurii*. Ed. James Willis. Leipzig, 1983.

Cassiodorus. *Cassiodori Senatoris Institutiones*. Ed. R. A. B. Mynors. Oxford, 1939.

Censorinus, *Censorini de die natali liber ad Q. Caerellium.* Ed. Nicholas Sallmann. Leipzig, 1983.

Diomedes. *Ars Grammatica.* Ed. H. Keil. Grammatici Latini 1. Leipzig, 1857.

Dionysius Thrax and the Technē Grammatikē. Ed. Vivien Law and Ineke Sluiter. Henry Sweet Society Studies in the History of Linguistics 1. Münster, 1995.

Donatus. *Ars Grammatica.* Ed. H. Keil. Grammatici Latini 4. Leipzig, 1864.

La Grammaire de Denys le Thrace. Ed. and trans. Jean Lallot. 2nd ed. Paris, 1998.

Grammatici Latini. Ed. H. Keil. 7 vols. Leipzig, 1855–1880.

Grammaticae Romanae Fragmenta. Ed. H. Funaioli. Stuttgart, 1969.

Hrabanus Maurus. *De clericorum institutione libri tres.* Ed. Detlev Zimpel. Freiburger Beiträge zur Mittelalterlichen Geschichte 7. Frankfurt am Main and New York, 1996.

———. *De universo.* PL 111.495–500.

———. *Excerptio de Arte grammatica Prisciani.* PL 111.613–678.

Hucbald of Saint-Amand. *L'oeuvre musicale d'Hucbald de Saint-Amand.* Ed. and trans. Yves Chartier. Montreal, 1995.

Isidore of Seville. *Isidori Hispalensis episcopi Etymologiarum sive originum libri XX.* Ed. W. M. Lindsay. Oxford, 1911; repr. 1966.

Laertius, Diogenes. *Lives of Eminent Philosophers.* Ed. Jeffrey Henderson, trans. R. D. Hicks. Loeb Classical Library. Cambridge, MA, and London, 1925; repr. 2000.

Macrobius. *Commentariorum in Somnium Scipionis Libri Duo.* Ed. Luigi Scarpa. Padua, 1981.

The Manual of Harmonics of Nicomachus the Pythagorean. Trans. and comm. Flora R. Levin. Grand Rapids, MI, 1994.

Marius Victorinus. *Marii Victorini Ars grammatica.* Ed. Italo Mariotti. Florence, 1967.

Murethach in Donati artem maiorem. Ed. Louis Holtz. Corpus Christianorum Continuatio Mediaevalis 40. Turnhout, 1977.

Musica Albini. In *Scriptores ecclesiastici de musica sacra potissimum,* ed. Martin Gerbert, 1:26–27. 3 vols. St. Blaise, 1784; repr. Hildesheim, 1963.

Musica et Scolica Enchiriadis una cum aliquibus tractatulis adiunctis. Ed. Hans Schmid. Munich, 1981.

Music Enchiriadis and Scolica Enchiriadis. Intro. and trans. Raymond Erickson. New Haven and London, 1995.

Musici Scriptores Graeci. Ed. Karl Jan. Hildesheim, 1962.

Plato. *Cratylus.* Ed. C. P. Goold, trans. Harold North Fowler. Loeb Classical Library. Cambridge, MA, and London, 1939; repr. 1992.

Plato. *Greater Hippias.* Ed. C. P. Goold, trans. Harold North Fowler. Loeb Classical Library. Cambridge, MA, and London, 1939; repr. 1992.

———. *Phaedrus.* Ed. E. H. Warmington, trans. Harold North Fowler. Loeb Classical Library. Cambridge, MA, and London, 1914; repr. 1971.

————. *Philebus.* Ed. G. P. Goold, trans. W. R. M. Lamb. Loeb Classical Library. Cambridge, MA, and London, 1925; repr. 1990.

————. *The Republic Books VI–X.* Ed. Jeffrey Henderson, trans. Paul Shorey. Loeb Classical Library. Cambridge, MA, and London, 1935; repr. 2000.

————. *Sophist.* Ed. G. P. Goold, trans. Harold North Fowler. Loeb Classical Library. Cambridge, MA, and London, 1921; repr. 1987.

————. *Theaetetus.* Ed. G. P. Goold, trans. Harold North Fowler. Loeb Classical Library. Cambridge, MA, and London, 1921; repr. 1987.

————. *Timaeus.* Ed. G. P. Goold, trans. R. G. Bury. Loeb Classical Library. Cambridge, MA, and London, 1929; repr. 1989.

Porphyry. *Porphyrios zur Harmonielehre des Ptolemaios.* Ed. Ingemar Düring. Göteborgs Högskolas Arsskrift 38. Göteborg, 1932.

Priscian. *Institutio grammatica.* Ed. H. Keil. Grammatici Latini 2–3. Leipzig, 1855.

Probus. *Instituta artium.* Ed H. Keil. Grammatici Latini 4. Leipzig, 1862.

Ptolemy, Claudius. *Die Harmonielehre des Klaudios Ptolemaios.* Ed. Ingemar Düring. Göteborgs Högskolas Årsskrift 36. Göteborg, 1930.

Quintilianus, Marcus Fabius. *The Institutio Oratoria of Quintilian.* Ed. G. P. Goold, trans. H. E. Butler. 4 vols. Loeb Classical Library. Cambridge, MA, and London, 1920; repr. 1989.

Regino of Prüm. *De harmonica institutione.* Ed. Edna Marie Le Roux, RSM. "The *De harmonica* and *Tonarius* of Regino of Prüm." Ph.D. diss., Catholic University of America, 1985.

Remigius of Auxerre. *In artem primam Donati.* Ed. W. Fox. Leipzig, 1902.

Sedulius Scottus. *In Donati artem minorem, In Priscianum, In Eutychem.* Ed. Bengt Löfstedt. Corpus Christianorum Continuatio Medievalis 40C. Turnhout, 1977.

Sextus Empiricus. *Against the Grammarians (Adversus Mathematicos I).* Ed. and trans. David L. Blank. Oxford, 1998.

Theon of Smyrna. *Theonis Smyrnaei Philosophi Platonici Expositio Rerum Mathematicarum ad Legendum Platonem Utilium.* Ed. Eduard Hiller. Leipzig, 1878; repr. New York and London, 1987.

Secondary Sources

Agawu, V. Kofi. *Playing with Signs: A Semiotic Interpretation of Classic Music.* Princeton, 1991.

Amsler, Mark. *Etymology and Grammatical Discourse in Late Antiquity and the Early Middle Ages.* Amsterdam, 1989.

Atkinson, Charles. *The Critical Nexus: Tone-System, Mode, and Notation in Early Medieval Music.* New York, 2008.

————. *"De Accentibus Toni Oritur Nota Quae Dicitur Neuma*: Prosodic Accents, the Accent Theory, and the Paleofrankish Script." In *Essays on Medieval Music in Honor of David G. Hughes*, ed. Graeme M. Boone, 17–42. Cambridge, MA, and London, 1995.

Backus, John. *The Acoustical Foundations of Music*. 2nd ed. New York and London, 1977.

Baddeley, Alan D. *Essentials of Human Memory*. Hove, 1999.

Banniard, Michel. *Genèse culturelle de l'Europe, Ve–VIIIe siècle*. Paris, 1989.

————. "Language and Communication in Carolingian Europe." In *The New Cambridge Medieval History*, vol. 2, *c.700–c.900*, ed. Rosamond McKitterick, 695–708. Cambridge, 1995.

————. "Latinophones, romanophones, germanophones: interactions identitaires et construction langagière (VIIIe–Xe siècle)." *Médiévales* 45 (2003): 25–42.

————. *Viva voce: Communication écrite et communication orale du IVe au IXe siècle en Occident latin*. Paris, 1992.

Barbera, André. "The Consonant Eleventh and the Expansion of the Musical Tetractys: A Study of Ancient Pythagoreanism." *Journal of Music Theory* 28 (1984): 191–223.

————, ed. *The Euclidean Division of the Canon: Greek and Latin Sources*. Lincoln, NE, and London, 1991.

Barker, Andrew, ed. *Greek Musical Writings*. Volume 2: *Harmonic and Acoustic Theory*. Cambridge, 1989.

————. *The Science of Harmonics in Classical Greece*. Cambridge, 2007.

Barrett, Sam. "Music and Writing: On the Compilation of Paris Bibliothèque Nationale lat. 1154." *Early Music History* 16 (1997): 55–96.

Belardi, Walter. *Filosofia grammatica e retorica nel pensiero antico*. Rome, 1985.

Bielitz, Mathias. *Musik und Grammatik*. Munich, 1977.

Bowen, C., and William R. Bowen. "The Translator as Interpreter: Euclid's *Sectio canonis* and Ptolemy's *Harmonica* in the Latin Tradition." In *Music Discourse from Classical to Early Modern Times: Editing and Translating Texts*, ed. Maria Rika Maniates, 97–148. Toronto, Buffalo, and London, 1990.

Bower, Calvin. "'Adhuc ex parte et in enigmate cernimus . . .': Reflections on the Closing Chapters of *Musica enchiriadis*." In *Music in the Mirror: Reflections on the History of Music Theory and Literature for the 21st Century*, ed. Andreas Giger and Thomas J. Mathiesen, 21–44. Lincoln, NE, and London, 2002.

————. "The Grammatical Model of Musical Understanding in the Middle Ages." In *Hermeneutics and Medieval Culture*, ed. Patrick J. Gallacher and Helen Damico, 133–45. Albany, 1989.

————. "The Transmission of Ancient Music Theory into the Middle Ages." In *The Cambridge History of Western Music Theory*, ed. Thomas Christensen, 136–67. Cambridge, 2002.

Carolingian Civilization: A Reader, ed. Paul Dutton. 2nd ed. Toronto, 2004.

Collart, J. *Varron grammairien latin*. Paris, 1954.

Contreni, John J. *Carolingian Learning, Masters and Manuscripts.* Aldershot and Brookfield, VT, 1992.

———. "The Carolingian Renaissance: Education and Literary Culture." In *The New Cambridge Medieval History*, vol. 2, *c.700–c.900*, ed. McKitterick, 709–57. Cambridge, 1995.

———. "The Pursuit of Knowledge in Carolingian Europe. In *The Gentle Voices of Teachers: Aspects of Learning in the Carolingian Age*, ed. Richard E. Sullivan, 106–41. Columbus, 1995.

Cook, Nicholas. "Epistemologies of Music Theory." In *The Cambridge History of Western Music Theory*, ed. Christensen, 78–105. Cambridge, 2002.

Crocker, Richard L. "Pythagorean Mathematics and Music." *Journal of Aesthetics and Art Criticism* 22 (1963): 189–98.

Diringer, David. *Writing.* London, 1962.

Eastwood, Bruce S. "Plinian Astronomical Diagrams in the Early Middle Ages." In *Mathematics and Its Application to Science and Natural Philosophy in the Middle Ages*, ed. Edward Grant and John P. Murdoch, 141–72. Cambridge, 1987.

Erickson, Raymond. "Eriugena, Boethius, and the Neoplatonism of *Musica* and *Scolia enchiriadis.*" In *Musical Humanism and its Legacy: Essays in Honor of Claude V. Palisca*, ed. Nancy Kovaleff Baker and Barbara Russano Hanning, 53–78. Stuyvesant, NY, 1992.

———. "Musica enchiriadis, Scolica enchiriadis." In *Grove Music Online. Oxford Music Online*, http://www.oxfordmusiconline.com/subscriber/article/grove/music/19405.

Flynn, William T. *Medieval Music as Medieval Exegesis.* Lanham, MD, 1999.

Fontaine, J. *Isidore de Séville et la culture classique dans l'Espagne wisigothique.* 3 vols. Paris, 1983.

Gelb, Ignace J. *A Study of Writing.* 2nd ed. Chicago, 1963.

Gentner, Dedre, and Michael Jeziorski. "The Shift from Metaphor to Analogy in Western Science." In *Metaphor and Thought*, ed. Andrew Ortony, 447–80. 2nd ed. Cambridge, 1993.

Godman, Peter. *Poetry of the Carolingian Renaissance.* Norman, OK, 1985.

Gushee, Lawrence A. "Questions of Genre in Medieval Treatises on Music." In *Gattungen der Musik in Einzeldarstellungen: Gedenkschrift Leo Schrade*, 365–433. Bern and Munich, 1973.

Haggh, Barbara. "Traktat *Musica disciplina* Aureliana Reomensis: Proweniencja i datowanie" ["*Musica disciplina* Aureliani Reomensis and the Problem of the Date and Origin of the Treatise"]. *Muzyka* 2 (2000): 25–78.

Hen, Yitzhak. "The Recycling of Liturgy under Pippin III and Charlemagne." In *Medieval Manuscripts in Transition: Tradition and Creative Recycling*, ed. Geert H. M. Claassens and Werner Verbeke, 149–60. Leuven, 2006.

———. *Royal Patronage of Liturgy in Frankish Gaul to the Death of Charles the Bald.* London, 2003.

Holtz, Louis. *Donat et la tradition de l'enseignement grammatical*. Paris, 1981.

Holyoak, Keith J., Dedre Gentner, and Boicho N. Kokinov. "Introduction: The Place of Analogy in Cognition." In *The Analogical Mind: Perspectives from Cognitive Science*, ed. Dedre Gentner, Keith J. Holyoak, and Boicho N. Kokinov, 1–20. Cambridge, MA, 2001.

Huglo, Michel. "Les diagrammes d'harmonique interpolés dans les manuscrits hispaniques de la *musica Isidori*." *Scriptorium* 48 (1994): 171–86.

———. *Les Tonaires: Inventaire, Analyse, Comparaison*. Paris, 1971.

Innes, Matthew. "Memory, Orality and Literacy in an Early Medieval Society." *Past and Present* 158 (1998): 3–36.

Intons-Peterson, Margaret Jean. "Components of Auditory Imagery." In *Auditory Imagery*, ed. Daniel Reisberg, 45–71. Hillsdale, NJ, 1992.

Irvine, Martin. *The Making of Textual Culture: 'Grammatica' and Literary Theory, 350–1100*. Cambridge, 1994.

Judd, Cristle Collins. *Reading Renaissance Music Theory: Hearing with the Eyes*. Cambridge, 2000.

Kaster, Robert. *Guardians of Language*. Berkeley, 1988.

Law, Vivien. "The Study of Grammar." In *Carolingian Culture: Emulation and Innovation*, ed. Rosamond McKitterick, 88–110. Cambridge, 1994.

Leech-Wilkinson, Daniel. *The Modern Invention of Medieval Music: Scholarship, Ideology, Performance*. Cambridge, 2002.

Levy, Kenneth. *Gregorian Chant and the Carolingians*. Princeton, 1998.

Masi, M. *Boethian Number Theory: A Translation of the* De institutione arithmetica. Amsterdam, 1983.

Mathiesen, Thomas J. "An Annotated Translation of Euclid's *Division of a Monochord*." *Journal of Music Theory* 19 (1975): 236–58.

———. *Apollo's Lyre: Greek Music and Music Theory in Antiquity and the Middle Ages*. Lincoln, NE, and London, 1999.

———. *Aristides Quintilianus: On Music in Three Books*. New Haven and London, 1983.

———. "Hermes or Clio? The Transmission of Ancient Music Theory." In *Musical Humanism and Its Legacy: Essays in Honor of Claude V. Palisca*, ed. Baker and Hanning, 3–35.

McKitterick, Rosalind. *The Carolingians and the Written Word*. Cambridge, 1989.

———. *Charlemagne: The Formation of a European Identity*. Cambridge, 2008.

Meyer, C. *Les traités de musique*. Typologie des sources du Moyen Âge occidental 85. Turnhout, 2001.

Miller, George A. "Images and Models, Similes and Metaphors." In *Metaphor and Thought*, ed. Ortony, 357–400.

Möller, Hartmut. "Zur Frage der musikgeschichtlichen Bedeutung der 'academia' am Hofe Karls des Grossen: Die *Musica Albini*." In *Akademie und*

Musik: Festschrift für Werner Braun zum 65. Geburtstag, ed. W. Frobenius et al., 269–88. Saarbrücken, 1993.

Music and Meaning. Ed. Jenefer Robinson. Ithaca and London, 1997.

Neisser, Ulric. "Changing Conceptions of Imagery." In *The Function and Nature of Imagery*, ed. P. W. Sheehan, 233–51. New York, 1972.

O'Donnell, J. R. "Alcuin's Priscian." In *Latin Script and Letters A.D. 400–900: Festschrift Presented to Ludwig Bieler*, ed. J. J. O'Meara et al., 222–35. Leiden, 1976.

Olsen, B. M. "Music in Western Education in the Early Middle Ages." In *Ars Musica–Musica Sacra*, ed. D. Hiley, 29–40. Tutzing, 2007.

Olson, David R. *The World on Paper: The Conceptual and Cognitive Implications of Writing and Reading.* Cambridge, 1994; repr. 1996.

Palazzo, Eric. *Liturgie et société au Moyen Age.* Paris, 2000.

Parkes, Malcolm. *Pause and Effect: An Introduction to the History of Punctuation in the West.* Berkeley and Los Angeles, 1993.

Petersen, Nils Holger. "Carolingian Music, Ritual, and Theology." In *The Appearances of Medieval Rituals: The Play of Construction and Modification*, ed. Nils Holger Petersen, Mette Birkedal Bruun, Jeremy Llewellyn, and Eyolf Østrem, 13–48. Turnhout, 2004.

Phillips, Nancy. "Classical and Late Latin Sources for Ninth-Century Treatises on Music." In *Music Theory and Its Sources: Antiquity and the Middle Ages*, ed. André Barbera, 100–35. Notre Dame, IN, 1990.

"Music." In *Medieval Latin*, ed. F.A.C. Mantello and A.G. Rigg, 296–306. Washington, DC, 1996.

———. "*Musica* and *Scolica Enchiriadis*: The Literary, Theoretical, and Musical Sources." Ph.D. diss., New York University, 1984.

Riché, Pierre. *Écoles et enseignement dans le Haut Moyen Age, fin du Ve siècle–milieu du XIe siècle.* Paris, 2000.

Ricoeur, Paul. *Interpretation Theory: Discourse and the Surplus of Meaning.* Fort Worth, 1976.

———. *Le mémoire, l'histoire, l'oubli.* Paris, 2000.

Saenger, Paul. *Space Between Words: The Origins of Silent Reading.* Stanford, 1997.

Scholes, Robert J., and Brenda J. Willis. "Linguists, Literacy, and the Intensionality of Marshall McLuhan's Western Man." In *Literacy and Orality*, ed. David R. Olson and Nancy Torrance, 215–35. Cambridge, 1991.

Sloboda, John. *The Musical Mind: The Cognitive Psychology of Music.* Oxford, 1985; repr. 1999.

Stock, Brian. *Listening for the Text: On the Uses of the Past.* Philadelphia, 1996.

Sullivan, Blair. "Alphabetic Writing and Hucbald's *Artificiales Notae*." In *Quellen und Studien zur Musiktheorie des Mittelalters*, vol. 3, ed. Michael Bernhard, 63–80. Munich, 2001.

————. "Grammar and Harmony: The Written Representation of Sound in Carolingian Treatises." Ph.D. diss., University of California, Los Angeles, 1994.

————. "*Nota* and *Notula*: Boethian Semantics and the Written Representation of Musical Sound in Carolingian Treatises." *Musica Disciplina* 47 (1993): 71–97.

————. "The Unwritable Sound of Music: Origins and Implications of Isidore's Memorial Metaphor." *Viator* 30 (1999): 1–21.

Teeuwen, Mariken. *Harmony and the Music of the Spheres: The Ars Musica in Ninth-Century Commentaries on Martianus Capella.* Leiden, Boston, and Cologne, 2002.

Treitler, Leo. *With Voice and Pen: Coming To Know Medieval Song and How It Was Made.* Oxford, 2003.

Vernant, Jean-Pierre. *Les origines de la pensée grecque.* 7th ed. Paris, 1997.

Veyne, Paul. *Les Grecs ont-ils cru à leur mythes?* Paris, 1983.

Vogt-Spira, Gregor. "Senses, Imagination, and Literature: Some Epistemological Considerations." In *Rethinking the Medieval Senses: Heritage / Fascination / Frames,* ed. Stephen G. Nichols, Andreas Kablitz, and Alison Calhoun, 51–72. Baltimore, 2008.

Waesberghe, J. Smits van. "La place exceptionnelle de l'Ars Musica dans le développement des sciences au siècle des carolingiens." *Révue grégorienne* 32 (1952): 81–104.

Warren, Richard M. *Auditory Perception: A New Analysis and Synthesis.* Cambridge, 1999.

Wright, R. "How Latin Came to Be a Foreign Language for All." In R. Wright, *A Sociophilological Study of Late Latin,* 3–17. Turnhout, 2002.

Zbikowski, Lawrence M. *Conceptualizing Music: Cognitive Structure, Theory, and Analysis.* AMS Studies in Music. Oxford, 2002.

Ziolkowski, Jan. *Nota Bene: Reading Classics and Writing Melodies in the Early Middle Ages.* Turnhout, 2007.